Seeing the body that had been in bed with her earlier took her breath away.

The shoulders and chest, which were broad but without bulk. The abdomen, which was flat yet rippled. Long arms, large hands. The leanly muscled legs of a triathlete.

She didn't want him to know she was there. Ridiculous when he'd probably sensed her stepping from the bed.

Still, he never said a word. And she never moved. Even when he looked up to see her half naked and staring.

He closed the refrigerator door then, silencing the room's grating light and returning the intimate darkness. She heard her own harsh breathing over the quiet, heard his, too, above his footsteps on the linoleum floor.

The rhythm of their heartbeats charged the air in the room, a deep throbbing beat older than man's soul. A powerful, telling beat that spoke of hunger and fear, of life and survival, of love and desperation.

IN DANGER

ALISON KENT

BRAVA

KENSINGTON PUBLISHING CORP.
http://www.kensingtonbooks.com

Contents

The
SHAUGHNESSEY
ACCORD

"With great power there must also come great responsibility!"
—Introducing Spider-Man

Amazing Fantasy #15, August 1962
Writer: Stan Lee
Artist: Steve Ditko
Original Price: $0.12
Near Mint Condition Price: $48,000

One

The Smithson Group's Manhattan ops center, never a hotbed of mind-blowing excitement in and of itself, was duller these days than a plastic knife working at a stick of cold butter.

It was driving Tripp Shaughnessey out of his ever-loving gourd.

He understood the laid-back, uneventful, mellow-as-molasses mood; really, he did. But without something to do besides sitting and staring zombie-eyed at static surveillance feeds, he was at a huge risk for losing the rest of his mind.

The Smithson Group—Christian Bane specifically—had recently pulled the plug and sent Peter Deacon, the sleazy front man for the international crime syndicate Spectra IT, swirling down one nasty drain.

That only left, oh, another umpty dozen members of the organization to annihilate.

There were days it seemed nothing short of an apocalyptic, second-coming, end-of-world scenario would make a dent in the work the SG-5 team had remaining to do.

In the meantime, Tripp's eyes and ass needed a break. Even a highly trained Smithson Group operative could only sit and stare for so long without giving in to distraction.

He pushed up from a squat to his feet, righted his chair, capped the tube of bearing grease he'd brought with him this morning, and tossed it to his desk.

He twirled the chair this way, twirled it that, sat and drew his knees to his chest.

Bracing the balls of his feet against the edge of his desktop, he shoved. The chair sailed into the center of the ops center's huge horseshoe-shaped workstation and beyond.

He was rolling, rolling, rolling . . . slowing, slowing, slowing . . .

"Crap."

He glanced to his right where Christian sat holding headphones to one ear, shaking his head.

He glanced to his left where Kelly John Beach faced him, arms crossed, brow arched.

Ooops.

"What the hell did I tell you? Inline-skate wheels, you moron. Otherwise, forget it. You can't race Hot Wheels on a NASCAR track."

Tripp shrugged, leaned back in his chair, legs extended, ankles crossed. It was all good. He had it under control.

Laced hands behind his head, he stared up into the cavernous darkness of the twenty-fourth floor's ceiling that was nothing but a web of exposed ductwork.

"Thought I'd give the bearing grease a try before changing out the wheels. Picked the stuff up at a skate shop down in Philly last week."

His comment was met with snorting in stereo, and Kelly John's, "Waste of money."

Tripp rolled his eyes. "Now, how can you say that when I bested my record by ten feet at least?"

"Good to see you're keeping yourself busy," Christian said without looking up.

K.J., on the other hand, met Tripp's gaze straight on. "Yeah, don't you have some work to do?"

"Nag, nag, nag." Yes, he had work to do. Or he would as soon as the Spectra IT agent he had on his scope made a noticeable move.

The agent who'd chosen Brighton's Spuds & Subs Sandwich Shop at the end of the block as his base of operations.

Tripp hadn't yet made the dude's cover story; he only knew the agent was monitoring the early afternoon traffic coming and going from the building across the street, housing, among other things, a privately held, family-owned-and-for-the-most-part-operated diamond exchange.

Tripp was monitoring the traffic as well. Especially since it wasn't Spectra's MO to deal with such a small-time operation as Marian Diamonds—and because word on the street said Marian Diamonds was trading in illegal conflict stones smuggled out of Sierra Leone.

Sure, the Spectra agent could've been canvassing the dealings of the entire block—a lot of high dollar transactions went on in the financial district between the hours of nine and five.

But just about the same time Spectra had shown up at Brighton's, the grandson of Marian's owner had gotten a hankering for sandwiches to eat long past lunchtime, ordering corned beef and sauer-kraut on rye to go the same time every afternoon.

Of course, his hankering could've been for Glory Brighton instead. In which case Tripp had a decision to make. Cement shoes or defenestration, because Glory Brighton was off-limits, whether she knew it or not.

His partners having put the kibosh on playtime, he spun his chair around and shoved off in the direction from which he'd come. This time he only made it two thirds of the way across the room.

Crap and a half.

He rolled his eyes. Christian chuckled. Kelly John offered up a round of applause and a suggestion. "Why don't you make yourself useful and go grab us some lunch?"

"I could. But I'm trying to keep a low profile here. Sticking with Hank's playbook and all that." Tripp followed the Smithson principal's instructions to the letter, but then so did all five of Hank's original handpicked operatives as well as the newest recruit.

Each one of them owed him, if not for the fact that their names weren't yet carved into nondescript tombstones, then for keeping them from a lot of years spent incarcerated at Leavenworth or Gitmo.

Besides, there was something about Hank's seventy-five years of experience at staying alive that spoke to a man.

"No one said you had to go to Brighton's," K.J. was saying. "Order a pizza. Pick up Chinese."

"Besides," Christian added, "there are other delis out there."

Tripp sputtered, feigning shock. "Heresy. Blasphemy. Other delis indeed."

K.J. waved Tripp away and turned back to the bank of monitors at his desk. "So, phone in an order. Have Glory leave it for you with Glenn in the garage. Pick it up there if you think your mark's gonna make you."

Tripp wasn't too keen on the idea. The garage separating the buildings housing Brighton's and Smithson Engineering—the cover for the SG-5 team—was no better than a war zone. The honking, the squealing tires, the exhaust fumes—not to mention the nosy punk parking attendant.

Forget getting in any quality Glory time with Glenn hovering around. And that quality time—even more than the freakish boredom—was the only reason Tripp was even considering venturing out of the ops center.

Kelly John and Christian might want food, but it wasn't too high on Tripp's list of priorities. He'd learned to do without in the weeks before Hank Smithson swooped down on salvation's wings and plucked him off a Colombian mountainside, and he'd never quite gotten back to his old way of thinking.

He ate enough to keep his body strong and able, his mind active and alert. Just not enough to start taking sustenance for granted. Not when he knew all too well the way life had of snatching away what he valued.

He glanced at the monitors on his desk. The first received the wireless feed from the camera hidden behind the marquee over the entrance to the Smithson Building. He toggled left, toggled right. Nothing out of the ordinary on the street in front of Brighton's or the diamond exchange.

Next he glanced at the monitor showing the feed from Brighton's security system. Glory had no knowledge of SG-5's video tap of her wires. The shop's surveillance cameras were simply set up to encourage employee honesty, scare straight the kids working for her, stuff like that.

But they told Tripp what he needed to know. Spectra IT's agent had not yet arrived.

Tripp pounced on the window of opportunity, shooting out of his chair and making like a rabbit for the door to the safety vestibule. The walls of the tiny chamber were constructed of sixteen-inch steel and separated the SG-5 nerve center from the floor's areas of public access.

"Back in a flash," he said, pressing his thumb to the pad of the biometric sensor. Mechanized bolts and pins disengaged and the door swung open.

"Or at least in an hour or two," Christian corrected.

"Hey. A girl likes a guy who takes his time," Tripp said, stepping inside. The closing door cut off further contact, sealing him up like a hot dog in Tupperware.

Overhead lights switched on inside the high-ceilinged, four-walled enclosure outfitted top to bottom in soundproofing tile.

Funny about that. The soundproofing. The lack of outside contact. How it still got to him after all this time. The idea of help being within reach . . . but not.

It wasn't like he needed help, or that he was really cut off, as seconds later he punched the code and exited into the suite's bamboo and black-lacquer façade of a reception area. And the confining space wasn't an issue.

But the idea of being on his own sure was enough to cause a bitch of a hitch in his side.

* * *

"Fourteen-seventy-eight, seventy-nine, eighty, ninety, fifteen and twenty." Glory Brighton counted out her customer's change. "There ya go, Wes. And you enjoy that new baby girl, ya hear?"

"No worries there, Glory," Wes said, lifting the white bag containing sandwich and chips in a parting gesture. "See you tomorrow."

"Yep. Same bat time, same bat sandwich," she said, and Wes chuckled. Oh, yeah. She was absolutely hilarious. Really cracked herself up. Snort.

Glancing at the phone then just as quickly away, she shut the register drawer, straightened the stack of expensive tri-fold color brochures and take-out menus on one side, closed up the display case of freshly baked and individually cellophaned cookies on the other.

Two-twenty-five apiece, and people paid without thinking twice. And why should she complain? They cost her a fraction of that and made for quite the tidy profit.

She wasn't complaining. Just . . . having a bad day. No real reason she should be. Except for the fight she'd had on the phone with her mother this morning.

Which meant that her father, having gone home for his Thursday lunch of a meat loaf sandwich and potato pancakes made from last night's leftovers, and by now on his way back to the bank, would be calling before he sat down for the afternoon to review loan applications.

Your mother has your best interests at heart, Glory. She is thinking of your future. Her concern for your welfare shows how very much she loves you.

Nothing in there about Ann Brighton's dread at

having to explain her only child's continuing lack of suitable matrimonial prospects to the ladies at the First Presbyterian Friday morning prayer circle.

The same group who two years later was still clucking over the fact that Glory had been taken in by that sweet-talking career criminal, Cody Scott, before he carjacked an undercover cop and got sent up the river to Riker's.

And nine months after the fact continued to sing a loud chorus of hallelujahs that she'd learned the truth of Jason Piaggi's affiliation with the "Piaggi Family" before it was too late.

Even now Glory couldn't help but roll her eyes. Such drama over nothing.

Yes. She'd made two bad man choices in her twenty-seven years. A girl was allowed a relationship strike or two, wasn't she? Before being written off as a has-been?

"Hey, Glory."

She glanced to the right, down the long sandwich bar where Neal Baker stood rewrapping the ham he'd sliced up for Wes.

"Hey, Neal."

He grinned, but not at her so much as at their personalized "hey, you" routine. "You still need me to hang around while you inventory for tomorrow's order?"

Shoot. The order. She'd been so focused on the inevitable call from her father that she was on the verge of a screw-up bigger than her penchant for dating criminal losers.

She untied her apron, slipped it off over her head. She knew Neal's girlfriend's dance troupe's showcase premiered tomorrow night and tonight was the family-and-friends preview.

"Sorry, Neal. I'll make it quick."

"Mikki appreciates it in advance."

"She damn well better," Glory teased, grabbing her clipboard from beneath the counter.

She made a quick visual sweep of the shop, took in the customers still eating, and glanced at the pickle-shaped wall clock.

Nothing going on Neal couldn't handle alone. Hell, his efficiency made the lack of hers that much more obvious. Ugh. There she went again with the ridiculous self-deprecation.

She was plenty efficient, she mused, heading into the storeroom down the hall at the rear of the shop. Just look at the shelves in here. A place for everything. Everything in its place.

It was just the constant parental haranguing that enforced the sense of being less. Less a good judge of character than expected of a daughter of Ann Brighton. Less respectable than what she would be as the married daughter of Milt.

And now with the trickle-down effect, she was feeling less efficient than her own part-time employee.

The only time lately she'd felt like *more* was when staring into the beautiful green eyes of one Smithson Engineering project consultant. That Tripp Shaughnessey. *Mmm-mmm-mmm.* Definitely one to throw a curve at a girl's plans.

Before he'd shown up in her shop weeks ago, months actually, though it seemed like days, seconds even, since she felt that first tingling rush of attraction every time he walked through her doors . . . before he'd shown up in her shop whenever it was, she'd been thinking of giving her parents' match-making efforts another chance, or two, or three.

Now she was thinking about nothing but having Tripp's babies. At least in a figurative sense.

Yes, she wanted to get married—eventually. Yes, she wanted to start her own family—when it was time. Yes, she wanted to test the proverbial boiling waters between Tripp and herself.

Right now, however, she needed to count the pickles so Neal could get going. The pickles, the olives, the paper napkins, the cans of tuna . . .

Could life possibly get any better than this? she mused.

And she was still musing ten minutes later when behind her the door to the storeroom slammed shut.

Two

Glory whirled around, hand pressed to the base of her throat. The click of the door latch still echoed as she stared at her intruder, glared at her intruder, watched as he reached down and turned the lock on the door, looking her way all the while.

Her gaze slid from his very large hand on the doorknob back to the face she saw every night in her dreams. She did her best not to sigh, to appear peeved rather than pleased, but it was hard when her tummy was tingling with blooming daffodil petals.

One eye narrowed, she pointed with the sharp end of her pencil. "You, Tripp Shaughnessey, are a very bad man."

"Ah, now, Glory, admit it. I'm not half as bad as you want me to be." He leaned his broad shoulders against the door, crossed his arms over his impressively buff chest, and grinned in that way he had.

That way that made her want to take off all of her

clothes, piece by piece in a slow sultry striptease—
a thought that sent the daffodil tingles tickling in
deep dark places that seemed these days to have
Tripp's name written all over them.

Returning her attention to the task at hand, she
finished counting the gallon cans of black olives,
marked her inventory sheet, then slipped the clipboard over the hook centered on the shelving
unit's support rail.

It was time, she decided, once she'd filled her
lungs with the air she needed to breathe. Time to
put her plan into motion. Or to take it to the next
level since she'd made the first move when she'd
dressed this morning with Tripp specifically in
mind.

She did that a lot these days.

"I dunno, Shaughnessey," she said, and turned.
"I'm not sure any man has it in him to be that
bad." She let her gaze crawl the length of his very
fine body, smoothing her palms over the zipped-
up and laced-up khaki miniskirt that hugged her
hips and little more.

He took in the motion of her hands; heat flared
in his bright green eyes. His thick honey-blond
lashes came down slowly, lifted in another smooth
upward sweep. His lips curved in a smile that said
oodles about all the ways he knew to be bad.

It was the very look she'd been hoping for, had
been waiting for, yes, had been planning for. She'd
seen it—no, she'd *felt* it—so many times lately but
never in the right place at the right time.

This, fingers crossed, could be both.

"Well, now. That sounds to me like a challenge,"
Tripp finally said after clearing his throat. He cocked
his head to the side and considered her. "And here

I thought you knew by now that I'm never one to back down."

She didn't know him at all. Not in the way she was determined to. In the way any woman would need to know the man she intended to become her intended as soon as she convinced him that he intended the same.

What she'd never counted on, however, was the sudden fluttering of nerves interfering with the daffodils and causing her to second-guess her brilliant master plan to seduce him, knock him senseless, leaving him desperate for more.

She thought of career criminals and mobsters and the First Presbyterian Friday morning prayer circle.

No. No second-guessing. It was now or never. She put her foot down on all her doubts, fortified herself with another monstrous nerve-settling breath, and took a step toward him.

"It's hard to get to know a guy when he sends his friends for his lunch." One step closer.

"When he can't even be bothered to order his own turkey, avocado, sprouts and Dijon." Another step, and nearer still.

"Or when he comes at lunch rush, and a girl can't spare a minute to flirt properly."

Tripp pulled in a deep breath, blew it out with a shake of his head. "Oh, Glory. If you don't think what you've been doing is properly . . ."

"So you like?" she asked, tilting up her chin just the tiniest, flirtiest bit.

He growled deep in his chest. "I'd like it a whole lot better if you'd give improperly a try."

She grinned, laughed under her breath, pushed a hand back through her mop of black curls and decided she might be able to pull this off after all.

"Thing is, Shaughnessey, for improperly I'm afraid I'm going to need a lot more help than you've been giving me."

His brow arched upward. He shifted his weight from one hip to the other. "That so?"

"Yeah. Definitely so."

She took her time closing the rest of the distance between them, not touching him, not quite yet, waiting for that, wanting to savor first contact. To press her lips to that dip in his collarbone and linger. To taste him. To breathe him in.

Her fingers itched to slip between the snaps of his pressed khaki shirt. Instead of following through, she glanced down and away from the pull of magic in his eyes. Her pink leather, wedged Mary Janes contrasted fiercely with his big bad, black motorcycle boots.

She was Red Riding Hood to his wolf. Little Miss Muffet to his spider. Wendy to his Peter Pan. He tempted her. He frightened her. She longed for him to sweep her away from the mundane and take her flying.

She was tired of making sandwiches and stuffing potatoes and inventorying supplies for reorder. Tired of having no social life except that arranged by her matchmaking parents who were determined she make a sensible match.

Sensible, schmensible. She wanted romance.

Again she sighed, allowed her gaze—now a slight frown—to climb up his long denim-clad legs to that place beneath his Adam's apple still tempting her so. "You dress like no engineering project consultant I know of."

"You know a lot of us engineering types, do you? To know what we should be wearing?" He uncrossed his arms, hooked his thumbs through two of his belt loops.

The move drew her attention the length of his torso, that long, strong, lean body that she ached to cuddle up to more than anything she'd wanted in a very long time. When had she grown so tired and so needy and so very enamored of this man?

"Obviously my education is lacking in the engineer's wardrobe department." This time she circled one fingertip around his topmost snap, there beneath that spot she was crazy to kiss. "You're welcome to enlighten me."

"Fieldwork," he said simply, as if he wasn't sure of his voice. "Boots and jeans when on-site. Suits and ties for the office."

"I see." She liked him in both, liked the urbane sophisticate with his debonair flare, that cool James Bond detachment, that hint of a smoldering fire.

But it was the clothes he wore today that got to her, that gave her hope. He could very well have been the boy next door she'd grown up with, building forts and selling lemonade and practicing the art of French kissing.

He seemed less out of her league, more approachable.

And so she approached, her finger moving to toy with the next button in the long row down. "So you're off into the field? To consult on a project? Would you like a sandwich for the road?"

"Actually, I'm just back," he said, his chest rising and falling more rapidly now. "I thought I'd stop in and see what you had to offer."

"Well," she began, dampening her pressed lips with the tip of her tongue. "The turkey is always fresh, and I just set out a new Cajun baked ham and a roast beef seasoned with sea salt."

"Hmm." He widened his stance, adjusted his weight, balanced on both feet. "I was thinking of something sweeter."

"I don't believe that for a minute, Shaughnessey. You never order dessert," she replied, certain that she would soon be unable to breathe, having lifted her gaze to meet his.

The twelve-by-twelve cinder block room shrank to the size of a matchbox. It didn't matter that they were surrounded by industrial steel shelving and metal lockers and enough ketchup to paint the town red. All she knew was that bad boy look in Tripp Shaughnessey's eyes.

Forget the fairy tales. He was Tarzan, she was Jane, and the heat of the jungle seethed.

"Oh, I don't know." His voice was low, a raspy whisper, rough and achingly raw. "I could go for a mouthful of cake right about now."

When he set his hands at her hip bones, she let him pull her forward, inching closer with tiny, sliding, baby steps until their bodies were flush. Her fingers returned to the first snap she'd toyed with, the first in the long row down . . . and *pop.*

"I have key lime cheesecake." *Pop.* Her heart blipped in her chest like a target on a radar screen. "Italian cream cake." *Pop.* She curled her toes in her shoes. "Fudge pecan pie." *Pop.* Her fingers shook. "Butter brownies and chocolate chip cookies." *Pop.* Her lungs deflated.

She pulled the tails of his shirt from his waistband and pressed eight fingertips to the first ridge of muscle delineating his abs. "Do any of those sound good?"

"I'm not so big on sugar."

She resisted letting her fingers drift lower to see if he was big on her. Instead, she tested the resilience of skin and muscle from his abs upward, stopping only when she reached his collarbone. Then, her index fingers found and measured that sexy little indentation she'd dreamed of kissing.

Frowning, she tapped him there. "Lean down a minute. You've got something right here . . ."

He did. And she did. And he tasted like heaven.

Tripp froze, an ice cube under assault from a blowtorch. Oh, Glory. Hot barely began to describe her. And it sure as hell didn't make a dent in explaining the temperature of her mouth.

He flexed his fingers at her hips where he held her, loving the give of her flesh, the nicely rounded curves that filled his hands with no poking from protruding bones.

He'd come in here to surprise her, to tease her, to steal a kiss or two or three. Yet he was the one now scrambling to recover. The one wondering if recovering was what he wanted to do.

He cleared his throat and swallowed. As expected, Glory lifted her head, and he asked, "Did you find what you were looking for?"

Her eyes grew sleepy, dreamy, and she nodded. "I did, yes, thanks."

She dropped her gaze to his chest, slid her palms from his pecs to his shoulders. He slid his hands from her hips around to cup her fine rump and handfuls of thick khaki skirt.

A smile stole along the edges of her mouth. He took it as encouragement and tugged her forward into the cradle of his lower body. "Hope you don't mind. Just making sure you're comfortable."

She wiggled a bit. "What about you?"

Oh, he was hard and beginning to ache and thinking it had been a long time since he'd found relief with a woman who tickled his fancy and not just his— "I'm good. Comfy. Still thinking about dessert."

"Well, I do have a special recipe. One I rarely share." She kneaded his shoulders beneath his shirt.

Her hands . . . he groaned, liking that "rarely" part a lot more than made sense. "Yeah? What might that be?"

"It's fairly rich. Definitely sweet." Her fingertips drifted to his armpits, down the underside of his arms until his sleeves caused resistance. "I'd call it . . . intense. The way it feels when a lemon torte hits your tongue."

He knew the feeling. A sizzling burst of too much too soon, which quickly gave way to wanting more. With Glory, he wanted more. He wanted to linger.

How many licks did it take to get to the center—

"Tripp?"

"Glory?"

"You've changed your mind, haven't you?"

Her question was spoken softly, hesitantly, as if she were bracing for rejection when he'd given her no reason to. He had no intention of turning her down or of letting her down.

He just wasn't sure this was the time or the place.

"Are you kidding?" He shook his head to reassure her, gathered up more of her short skirt's fabric until his fingertips brushed the flesh beneath. He had a hell of a time swallowing his responding groan. "I was just thinking it might be nice to start with an appetizer."

"I think that's what we're doing," she said, looking up at him then from beneath a fringe of jet black lashes.

He chuckled. He liked that he hadn't scared her away. It was always a matter of balance, of taking his time as he tested the waters.

He gave a playful smack of his lips. "I'm not so sure. I'm not tasting anything here."

Her roaming fingers found the edges of his shirt, closed around the fabric, used his collar as a handle to pull his head down and press her mouth to his.

Three

She'd known by looking at his mouth that he'd be a wonderful kisser. She'd listened when he'd talked, watched the way he'd held his lips when considering what he wanted to order.

She'd known, but she hadn't known at all, because he kissed like Tripp and like no one else at all.

He was gently demanding, his hands having moved from her bottom to her head, the heels of his palms at her cheeks, his fingers threading into her hair as he held her.

Held her and kissed her as if she were the only woman in the world he wanted to kiss, the only one who mattered.

She loved the daffodil tingles sweeping through her body, loved the feel of his lips. The soft searching, the sweet nudging press as he urged her mouth open and slipped his tongue inside.

She released his shirt collar, moved her palms to his chest, enjoyed the dusting of hair there that tickled. He was lean, possessed with the type of body that seemed to thrive on less sustenance than more. Of that she was certain because of how little he ordered; she had often wondered how much of what he bought and paid for he actually ate.

His ribs lay beneath the same sleek muscle that rippled over his abdomen. She touched him there, explored all she could reach of his bare skin, setting loose a feral growl that rose in a rumbling wave from his belly up his throat.

His kiss grew demanding, grew hungry, as if what he needed right now in this moment were things only she had to offer. If he only knew how much there was, how deep ran her longing to give . . .

"Oh, Glory," he pulled his mouth free to mumble. "You amaze me."

"Why's that?" she mumbled right back, her lips brushing his cheek, his jaw, over his chin. "I'm not so amazing, really."

He chuckled. "Oh, yes. You are. Especially the way you do that. Right there."

"This?" she asked, her thumbs circling his navel like finely meshed gears. One clockwise, one counter, around and around and around.

He shuddered, clenched the muscles beneath her hands, nuzzled the skin under her jaw with his nose and his mouth, a little bit of teeth.

Heaven. Pure heaven. Absolute bliss. She couldn't conceive of anything better even knowing how much of the unknown remained to be discovered.

She slipped a hand around Tripp's waist, found the doorknob, made sure he'd turned the lock all the way . . .

The Verizon telephone panel van pulled into the alley behind the sandwich shop having made a final circle of the long city block.

The six men inside each wore identical black warm-up suits, athletic shoes, leather gloves and ski masks. All logos and labels had been stripped from the clothing, rendering each item as generic as was possible.

Each man carried the same Beretta 9mm. The guns no longer bore traceable serial numbers. None of them had ever been fired. Not in a crime, nor for fingerprinting by any firearms manufacturer. Not a single ballistics marking existed in any database.

The van had been jacked while the service tech took his lunch break. He now lay blindfolded, gagged and trussed like a Butterball on the van's floor, but would be back on the clock in less than thirty minutes.

It would take the men half that long to get in and out of Brighton's though they'd been drilled to do it in less.

Danh Vuong wasn't the least bit worried about getting caught. He'd covered every base, taken every precaution. If anything came up, his men would adjust, improvise. They'd been drilled, too, to think on their feet.

No one working for Son Cam survived long without that particular skill, and Danh had been working for the man for close on twelve years now.

A dozen winters spent wearing Italian leather, cashmere and wool.

A dozen summers spent driving German luxury cars, riding in air-conditioned interiors behind bulletproof glass.

Danh was a far cry and a continent away from the stowaway wharf rat who'd made his way to the Los Angeles harbor via container ship, who'd crossed the grand ole U.S. of A. using his wits, his brains, his two hands and his mouth in ways a ten-year-old boy should never have had to do.

New York City had been his destination. No other location existed. He had plans. Big plans. And the past that had brought him here was now a very small memory. One he'd locked away and left to wither and die.

Danh double-checked the contents of his pockets. His cell phone was a prepaid throwaway he would use only should he run out of options. The zip ties would guarantee his safety as well as that of any bystander he was forced to restrain.

His contact at Marian Diamonds had gone mute, and had done so at the same time the Spectra IT syndicate had begun trespassing on Mr. Cam's business. It was an unsatisfactory state of affairs, one Danh intended to correct today.

During the last circle the van had made around the block, he'd seen the Spectra agent enter Brighton's. By the time the traffic signal at the corner had changed, the contact from Marian's had come and gone.

Danh was having none of it. Mr. Cam had given Danh a home when he had none, an education when he'd thought he'd never read, the food and clothing he'd wondered how to pay for.

He'd offered to pay in the same way he'd paid for his trip to New York from L.A. Mr. Cam had declined, teaching Danh his first real lesson.

With a family behind you, you were never on your own. Even if said family shared no blood but that which bound their oath.

Though Glory had double-checked the lock on the storeroom door, Tripp hesitated, uncertain whether she was keeping him in or keeping everyone else out. It was a subtle distinction that he doubted a lot of guys would make, but then, he overanalyzed on a regular basis.

That trait remained at odds with his tendency to take very little seriously, but it was the one that had drawn Hank Smithson's attention while the older man was busy boning up on the facts of Tripp's imminent court-martial—a future he himself had pondered while on the run from his own superiors in Colombia.

How Hank had gotten his hands on Tripp's *Top Secret* records remained a mystery the older man would take to his grave. Not a one of the SG-5 team members knew how or why he'd found and saved their sorry hides. Not a one of them really cared. The fact that he had was all that mattered.

Just like the fact that Glory had locked the storeroom door was all that mattered here.

Tripp moved his hands from her face, settled them on her shoulders, did his best to ignore the sensation of her fingertips flirting with his skin. It was hard when she flirted so sweetly, teasing him and tempting him there above his belt.

If he didn't ignore what was happening below, however, he'd be back at the ops center eating his lunch and wondering why the hell he hadn't savored this sweet opportunity to have dessert first.

Sweet. Oh, Glory. That's exactly what she was. Purely sweet. Her mouth, her fingers, her coffee-bright eyes when she looked up while brushing his collarbone with feather-light kisses.

He shuddered, kneaded her shoulders, whispered, "Amazing."

She chuckled, still kissing his chest and shaking

her head. "Mandarin cream chocolate torte is amazing. Raspberry silk truffles rolled in powdered hazelnuts are amazing. I'm just Glory."

"You make my mouth water."

"That's what desserts are supposed to do."

He dropped his head back on the door and pulled in a breath he hoped would ground him back in the world of meat and potatoes. It wasn't happening. He was dying here. She was killing him sweetly, softly.

He'd stop if she said to. Only if she said to. But she didn't say a thing. One more deep breath and he pushed off the door, backed her into the wall at the right, spread her thighs with the knee he wedged between, and kissed her madly, feeling the thundering beat of her pulse where he cupped the base of her throat.

He sent his other hand exploring lower, down between their bodies to the hem of her skirt and her legs that he'd parted. He found her panties. Cotton. As soft as her kisses, as were the plump lips of her sex swollen beneath. He slipped a finger under the elastic at the crease of her leg.

She gasped into his mouth at the contact. He swallowed the sound, nudging his knuckle upward through her folds. Her fingers dug into his biceps. He feared she would push him away, that he'd gone too far, and readied himself to stop.

She pulled him closer instead, holding on while she whimpered, tipping her lower body upward, asking for the more that he so wanted to give her with body parts other than his fingers or thumb.

Time and place, man. Time and place.

He continued to kiss her, continued to play her, eating up her cries and whimpers the way he wanted to eat up the rest of her. He could taste the change in her, the salty electric tingle along her tongue, and knew she was close to coming.

He wanted to take her there, to give her this pleasure. She was so damn candy sweet, so vibrant, so open. It was a wonder he'd been able to keep his distance at all. He doubted he'd ever keep it again.

And here he'd been so good for so long, swearing off dessert, knowing how bad it was for him. But when Glory tore her mouth from his and whispered his name, when she closed her eyes and gave herself up to his touch, it was a surrender that knocked him breathless.

Her entire body shuddered; he felt her tremors where his limbs were tangled in and out of hers, where his torso held hers pinned to the wall, where his fingers eased her down from the high.

He watched her lashes flutter as she opened her eyes and slowly turned her head to look at him, watched her press her lips together, then bathe them with her tongue.

He pulled his hand from her panties, wishing he could linger and give her even more. But his pants were too tight and he had to get back to work and, ah, hell, a storeroom was no place to make serious love to this woman. Not in all the ways he wanted to.

She moved her hands up and pushed her thick mop of black curls from her face. She smiled then, as she looked at him and said, "Wow."

He grinned right back. "Good stuff, huh?"

She pulled in a deep, steadying, satisfied breath. "Lemon tortes have nothing on you, Shaughnessey."

He tossed back his head and laughed. This one was going to be a hell of a lot of fun to get to know better.

A hell of a lot of fun.

Danh ordered his men out of the van with no more than a wave of his hand. Footsteps fell soundlessly in the alley. The vehicle's doors closed without a creak. He waited for the five to fall in behind him, pressed to the building's wall, before he eased open the sandwich shop's back door.

He knew from earlier surveillance that they would be stepping into a small hallway that serviced the shop's restrooms and storeroom. The goal was to make it into the main shop undetected. Once there, phase two of the plan would be set into motion.

Right now, however, it was time to complete phase one.

He slipped through the door behind his number one man, Qua^n, standing guard while the other man checked both rest-rooms—empty—and the storeroom—locked—before blacking out the shop's security camera with spray paint.

Danh then signaled for the rest of his men to enter, left Qua^n at his post in the back hallway. He knew there were no scheduled deliveries the rest of the afternoon. Unscheduled, he had to cover for.

At his command, his four men spread out through the sandwich shop on catlike feet. Gasps and screams were cut off rapidly with a single wave of a weapon as Danh motioned the sole employee and five customers to gather at the rear of the shop.

Behind him, his men went to work lowering the blinds on the front windows, the ones covering the main door, the set hanging over the rear exit into the garage. The signs on both doors were turned to "Closed." The locks were secured as well.

Good. Done. Now to get what he had come for.

"Ladies and gentlemen, good afternoon. We will take no more than a few minutes of your time, then be on our way. If you will each stand and place your hands behind you, my men will secure both your safety and ours."

"Just take the money from the till and get the hell out of here."

Danh turned his attention to the young man wearing the name tag and the brown apron with Brighton's green-and-yellow logo. "If we were here for the money, Neal, we would be gone by now. Face the wall. Hands at your back. Everyone but you, sir, in the tweed sport coat."

Two of Danh's men quickly circled the hostages' wrists with zip ties. A third spaced out chairs against the side wall and settled their captives as comfortably as possible. The fourth of his men, along with Danh himself, ushered the Spectra agent into the shop's hallway.

Danh circled him slowly, taking in the costume of wool, cashmere and tweed, the ink-stained fingertips, the brown leather journal he still held tucked beneath his arm. The tiny gold-framed spectacles completed the picture, giving the agent the look of a scholar, a writer, the perfect cliché.

"Professor Shore, correct?" Danh queried, appreciating the brief flash of anger before the other man's features settled into an expression of fearful concern more appropriate to the situation.

The agent cleared his throat. "If you'll return the use of my hands, I'll gladly give you my money clip, my watch, anything you want."

Danh admired the man's absorption in his role. Spectra IT trained their agents well. "I am not interested in your money or your possessions, Professor. What I want is something that interests only you and I. Once you turn it over to me, I will release all of you and be on my way."

"You ain't going nowhere, dickhead."

Danh turned at the rudely shouted challenge and stepped back to view the customers lined up like a shooting gallery's ducks. "You, sir. You plan to stop me?"

"You bet your sweet bippy. Me and my brothers in blue. You've heard of New York's finest? I'm off duty." He indicated the phone hooked to his belt at his waist. "This baby's been transmitting to 9-1-1 since you and your Halloween parade started marching around."

Danh nodded to his nearest associate who removed the cell from the officer's belt and nodded. A sharp stirring of unease had Danh clamping down on saying more. After all, silence intimidated far greater than swagger. His temples throbbing, he simply inclined his head.

His man sent the hostage to the floor with a blow from the butt of his gun. The two female customers screamed, whimpered, sobbed. Danh's man acted automatically, quieting them both with duct tape before taking up his position again.

Ignoring the tic at the corner of his eye, Danh returned to his interrogation. Seconds later, a bullhorn outside sounded with a loud, "This is the police!"

The tic grew impossible to ignore. Now Danh was facing the only contingency he'd never planned for.

A standoff.

Four

"What the hell was that?" Tripp jerked his head away from Glory's and toward the storeroom's locked door. He stepped back while she smoothed down her shirt, adjusted her skirt and her panties.

Frowning, she followed the direction of his gaze. "It sounded like"—he pressed a silencing finger to his lips; she lowered her voice—"a police bullhorn."

"Yeah. That's what I was thinking." He held out a halting hand. "Stay where you are."

"Uh, okay," she said, agreeing like the good little girl who followed orders he obviously thought she was when what she really wanted to do was move the hell away from the one and only entrance into the room. "How long do you want me to stay?"

He didn't answer. Instead, he backed his way across the concrete floor, his gaze trained on the door until he reached the corner and the built-in, fireproof safety cabinet holding her safe, her files, and her security system's equipment.

She watched, mouth agape, as he twirled the dial on the cabinet's combination lock and opened the door. She was done standing still. "What the hell are you doing?"

"Shit. Your camera's down."

"What?" What the hell was going on here? "Look, Shaughnessey. You tell me how the hell you know my combination, not to mention where my monitor is . . ." She peered around his shoulder at the small television on top of the VCR recording the store camera's data.

He was wrong. The camera wasn't down. She could see movement in one corner. The rest of the lens had been blacked out by spray paint judging by the speckles peppering the missed spot. "I'm calling the cops."

"No," Tripp barked, but she'd already backed away and lifted the handset from the phone on the wall.

"It's dead." She held it out, away from her ear, wondering if the second line in the shop was still working.

Tripp nodded but kept his attention on the coaxial cable running into the back of the TV.

She hung up the useless phone, told herself she was in good hands, that she could trust him, even while a tiny voice reminded her that she didn't know him well enough to jump to that conclusion.

The things he was doing, the knife he'd pulled from his pocket, the fact that he was cutting into the cable . . .

She crossed the room, grabbed the wrist of the hand holding the knife, the hand he'd used to make her come, and stared him in the eye. "You tell me what's going on and tell me now or so help me—"

"What? So help you what? You'll run out the door into who knows what?" He pulled back the cable's black covering, shredded what looked like a coating of woven fabric around the core copper wire. "Stay put. That's all I'm asking."

She didn't want to do anything he said, not when he'd suddenly clammed up. Not when everything he was doing was as underhanded and sneaky—if not downright illegal—as anything that would bring out cops with bullhorns.

But staying put was what she ended up doing because she had no better idea. She looked on as Tripp twisted a short strip of the shredded fabric and tapped it against the copper. Three short taps, three long, three short.

An obvious SOS.

"Are you trying to signal the security company?" And why, with the police already outside? "I don't pay for twenty-four/seven monitoring. No one is going to hear that."

"They're not supposed to hear it."

Glory rubbed a hand to her tense forehead. This was getting worse by the second. "What, then? See it? How can they see it?"

"It's not your security service I'm trying to reach." He glanced sharply from the static on the blacked-out feed to the door, his brows drawn down into a deep V. "Can you take over? Three short, three long—"

"Three short. My degree might be in business, but I did learn your basic SOS."

"Good girl," he said.

She wanted to snap and growl at his use of "girl" but, quite frankly, she was too damned worried. Flat-out scared, if the truth be known, taking the cable from his hands.

Scared and suddenly longing for one of the safe-and-so-what-if-he's-boring dates of her parents' choosing. She wanted to be anywhere but here with this obviously dangerous man who turned her on, burned her up, then betrayed her by breaking into her not-so-secure security system.

She tapped the twisted fabric to the wire, felt a strange metallic tang in her teeth, wondered who the hell it was she was signaling. And, at the same time, sending out vibes to her mother's First Presbyterian prayer circle that she wasn't shorting out her only route of escape.

Sweat ran between Tripp's shoulder blades and pooled at the base of his spine. He'd been in such a hurry to get to Glory that he'd left his cell on his desk charging. Meaning, having it with him wouldn't have done him a fat lot of good anyway seeing as how it was dead.

He needed to reach the ops center, let Christian or Kelly John know something was going down. One of them ought to get hungry enough soon to realize he hadn't returned. Logic told him they'd check his monitor showing the Brighton feed, see the SOS static, and realize he had a situation here on his hands.

He trusted his partners to get him and Glory out. He trusted the cops out front to bungle whatever it was they were doing. Nothing particular against New York City's finest. His beef was with authority figures in general, letting power go to their heads, twisting the law to suit their purpose, lifting themselves above it.

Sorta the way things had gone down in Colombia, leaving him facing the short stick of a court-

martial for desertion—a way-the-hell-better scenario than sticking around to face certain death
after blowing the whistle on the drug deals his superiors had been making in the name of the law.

With Glory looking on, not looking happy
about what he'd asked her to do but at least looking like she wouldn't give up, he twisted the lock
on the door as quietly as he could. Next, he turned
the handle, cracked the door open and braced the
bulk of his body for an inward attack.

Nothing.

His knife at the ready, he moved his head far
enough to peer with one eye through the sliver of an
opening, seeing nothing but the brown-and-yellow
textured wallpaper and the edge of one of the shop's
signature black-framed prints.

A centimeter wider, and this time the glimpse of
black he caught belonged to what looked like the
sleeve of a jacket. He shifted to his other eye, got
nothing but the same perspective, and so cracked
the door open further.

This time it was enough. He heard snuffling
and whimpering and then an indistinctive voice—
no accent, no inflection—calmly say, "Our friends
outside are not going to deter me, Professor. I plan
to be gone before they begin their textbook driven
negotiation process to secure the safe release of
our hostages."

Hostages! Shit!

"I would be more than happy to oblige"—this
from a second, distinctly cultured voice—"if I had
an inkling as to what you were talking about."

Tripp couldn't identify the players. The voices
were unfamiliar. He had no clue as to what was
happening. He only knew that he had to stop
whatever it was.

The black sleeve shifted enough for him to see a slice of a head in a black ski mask. Again, no way to identify who or what he was up against without getting closer. He pushed the door closed without a sound, backed his way across the room to where Glory stood.

She stared at him, eyes wide and liquid though she hadn't shed a tear. She still held the cable he'd handed her, though at some point she'd stopped tapping out the SOS. It was good enough. One of his partners would eventually notice the problem with the Brighton feed.

Once they rewound the tape to find out when what had gone down, they'd devise a rescue plan in a hurry. But he couldn't wait around for any of that to happen. He wanted Glory safely out of here now. Even if he had to rely solely on himself.

He took the cable from her hands, moved her to the same spot she'd stood in before, before when he'd kissed her, when he'd made her come with his hand. "I want you out of sight in case anyone comes charging through the door."

"You want me to stay put, you mean."

"If something happens to you, I'll never forgive myself for not gorging on dessert when I had the chance."

She blinked hard to keep away the tears. "You are so not funny, Shaughnessey."

"No, but you're crazy about me anyway."

"Don't count on it."

"I've been counting on it for weeks already," he said with a wink. And then he sobered. "I need to find out what's happening. I don't want to put you in more danger than you already are, but I have to do this."

"Do what?" she pleaded in a whisper. "Why

don't you just let the police handle it? I think
we're safe. No one knows we're here."

"It won't take them five seconds to find out. I'd
like to know who we're dealing with here should
that happen."

"*We're* not dealing with anyone, Tripp. Please let
the police handle it. This is what they're trained to
do."

What was he going to tell her? That he didn't
trust the police? That he was better trained than
the good guys on the bullhorn but he wouldn't
know about the bad guys until he took a closer
look?

He finally asked her to simply, "Trust me? I'm
not going to do anything stupid."

She gave him a look in return that said she
wouldn't trust him half as far as Gary Sheffield
could throw a baseball. So he held her fingers in
his, brought them to his mouth and kissed her
knuckles. Then he gave her a grin meant to tell
her to leave all the worry to him.

He took his time cracking the door open again.
The sleeve and ski mask obviously belonged to a
lookout. The shop's back hallway was only accessible by those already in the shop or those using the
alley's door. Meaning, whoever was making demands inside wanted new arrivals kept out and
everyone else kept in place.

He took a deep breath, not sure if he was tamping down or revving up the adrenaline, nodded at
Glory, and that was it. He pulled open the door.
One long step into the hallway. A hand clamped
over the guard's mouth. Pressure applied to a
point just below his carotid.

The man was dead to the world from the choke
hold before he even knew what hit him. And

deader than deadweight as Tripp dragged him into the storeroom. Glory eased the door closed behind them. No more than a few seconds had passed. No real noise made. Tripp planted a knee in the small of the man's back.

He didn't bother with the ski mask yet but emptied all the pockets, finding the two things he'd most wanted to find. A 9mm Beretta and a cell phone.

He tucked the gun into his waistband, punched a number into the phone that no government agency would ever be able to trace, and once connected said, "Shaughnessey."

Several minutes later, a computerized voice replied, "Thank you," signaling that his location had been made.

five

Once the biometric sensor read the scan of Julian Samms's thumbprint, the ops center's door slid open. He stepped out of the safety vestibule and into the cavernous room, the hub of SG-5's activities.

Christian and Kelly John both looked up. One nodded. One lifted a hand in greeting. Tripp wasn't anywhere to be seen. Eli McKenzie, the fifth member of the original team, had recently returned to the field in Mexico, having recovered from a nasty— and suspicious—poisoning.

"Where's Shaughnessey?" Julian asked, heading for his own desk to download the files he'd need in Miami where he was headed later today. Ostensibly to save a woman's life.

What he'd learned about her made him more ambivalent than was wise when prepping for a mission. But this one had tied herself to Spectra IT willingly, and he didn't have a lot of sympathy for anyone that dumb.

K.J. pushed away from his desk, swiveled his

chair toward Tripp's corner of the workstation, and frowned. "He went for lunch. Like thirty minutes ago."

Typing his security code into the system, Julian snorted. "He go back to Philly for cheesesteaks, or what?"

This time it was Christian who pushed out of his chair. "He went to Brighton's. Check the feed. See if he's still over there messing with Glory. He did say something about taking his time."

The three Smithson operatives gathered in front of Tripp's desk, K.J. finally settling into the chair when it became clear that the camera broadcasting from Brighton's was broadcasting nothing but snow.

Julian and Christian watched as Kelly John checked the input and output connections, finding nothing wrong with the equipment, and queued the last thirty minutes of recorded feed to play.

"Jesus H. Christ." Christian picked up the phone on Tripp's desk five minutes later. "Hank needs to see this."

This being a blast of black spray paint out of nowhere followed by pulses of static that were an obvious SOS.

Christian dialed. Kelly John ground his jaw until it audibly popped. Julian switched to mentally cursing in Mandarin.

It was when the phone on the tracking computer buzzed across the room to signal a trace, that all three men turned.

And all three men started to sweat.

Hank Smithson stood in the wide triangle of space behind his desk and in front of his L-shaped credenza. His corner office on the twenty-third floor of the Manhattan financial district high-rise offered a view to beat all views.

He just wasn't in much of a mood to be viewing. Dad-blamed office work. He wanted to be back in Saratoga on the farm, watching MaddyB take a turn around the track, listening to the wind blowing down, and breathing in the smell of the Adirondacks.

Else he wanted to be upstairs, he mused wistfully, glancing toward the ceiling and wondering if he could get away with at least taking over a bit of the surveillance Tripp Shaughnessey was doing these days without his boys huffin' and puffin' about him needing to take it easy.

"Mr. Smithson?"

Easy was for wimps. Hank walked over to punch the intercom on his desk. "Yes, Emma?"

"I'm heading out for lunch. Can I bring you anything?"

Emma Webster. His secretary. Nope. Administrative assistant, she insisted on being called. A good woman. One of a very few he'd known in his life. "I'm fine. Ate too big of a breakfast this morning."

"If you're sure?"

"Yes, ma'am. I'm sure." He pictured the twitch of her perky nose. She hated to be called ma'am. "But, Emma? When you get back, will you find Jackson Briggs for me?"

"I'm sorry. Did I forget an appointment?"

He heard the fluster in her voice as she tried to recall any previous request he'd made for his chopper pilot's services. "Not at all. I was just thinking I might like to get back to the farm a couple days early is all."

"Let me get him for you now."

Hank shook his head, grinning to himself, thinking how much his Madelyn would've enjoyed Emma's dedication, the way she thought of everyone around her before ever thinking of herself. "You go on to lunch. Briggs will be around when you get back."

"Yes, sir. I'll be back in thirty minutes."

And she would be, too. The girl was always true to her word. He and Madelyn had never been blessed with children, but he would've enjoyed having a daughter like Emma.

Much as he could've seen himself as father to the five boys who made up the core of his Smithson Group, spending their days going where law-abiding, rule-stickling, by-the-bookers wouldn't and getting done what needed to get done.

Doing it all these days without him, of course, which grated on his nerves as much as the shrapnel he'd taken during Operation Just Cause in Panama continued to grate on his dad-blamed hip.

He needed to get out of here. He really did. He thought long and hard about ruining Emma's afternoon and raising Briggs himself while standing there, fiddling in his desktop humidor for one of his favorite Montecristo Corona Grandes, needing something to do.

And if that wasn't just the crux of it all, his needing something to do.

The thought was still on his mind, the wrapper still on his cigar, when the private line in the lower left desk drawer rang.

Tripp pocketed the cell phone that looked like a cheap throwaway without saying a word. He'd made a call but he hadn't spoken beyond saying his name.

Glory wasn't sure if she should start fuming now or wait for his lame excuses explaining away what looked like a lot of unlawful activity an engineering project consultant had no business engaging in.

Especially disconcerting was Tripp's way too familiar familiarity with the handgun he'd taken off the other man.

She watched now as he removed what she thought was called a clip, checked it for bullets before putting it back together and tucking it into his waistband beneath the right side of his shirt.

"Why not in the small of your back?" She gestured uselessly toward him. Uselessly because he wasn't even looking at her.

"Easier access on the side. Movies don't always get it right, you know."

No. She didn't know. And how the hell did he? "Just who the hell *are* you, Tripp? Or should I say, *what* are you?"

He did glance up then. "That's a conversation best had another time. Right now I need tape or twine or both. Whatever you've got back here to immobilize this one."

She had tape and twine both, found a roll and a spool in the same cabinet as her security system and handed them off. Tripp bound the man's hands and feet, pulled off his ski mask and taped his mouth.

"Anyone you know?" Tripp asked.

The young Asian didn't stand out at all in her mind, and she shook her head. "Do you still want me to send the SOS?"

Tripp dragged the unconscious man to the center of the room. "No. If they were going to pick up the signal, they would've done so by now."

"Who are *they*?"

"Friends of mine." He returned to the door.

She glanced down at the other man, a kid, really, lying between them. "Don't you want him out of the way?"

"I want him where he can't kick over any of your shelves if he wakes up while I'm otherwise occupied."

"Occupied doing what, exactly?" She hated feeling left out when she was up to her eyeballs involved. "It would be nice if you'd let me in on what's going on here seeing as how this is my shop and all."

"Glory, sweetheart. I swear I'll tell you everything. Just not right now."

"So, I stay put." Ugh, but that grated. Not that she would have a clue how to get herself out if he wasn't here.

"Staying put would be great, thanks."

She felt useless, worthless, scared in so many ways she was numb with it. But she still had to fight the urge to stick out her tongue at his back. "Okay, but do you have a plan? What do I need to do while you're doing whatever it is you're doing?"

She heard Tripp sigh, but it wasn't a sound of exasperation. More like a sound of patient resignation. He glanced at her, admiration warming his eyes. Seeming to register all of what she was feeling, he moved from the door to cup her face in his hands.

"I'm sorry. I wish like hell this wasn't happening, that you weren't having to go through this. I'm operating here on auto-pilot, and I'm not used to making explanations. I need you to trust me."

Autopilot? Explanations? She focused on the one crazy truth that she knew. "I do trust you. What do you want me to do?"

"Oh, Glory." He tickled her with a teasing laugh. "If you only knew."

"Try me."

His gaze heated possessively. "I intend to, in every way possible. As often as possible." He let that sink in a simmering moment before adding, "After you're safe."

Too late, Glory thought. *I'm already a goner.*

After a long moment, one tense with all the things unspoken between them, he lowered his hands and took a step back. "It's not a big deal, really. Just my military training rearing its ugly head."

"You were in the military? Before Smithson Engineering?" There were so many things about him she didn't know, wanted to learn, wondered if she'd ever have the chance.

He nodded. "Same route a lot of guys take when they're clueless as to their future."

He said it blithely enough that she didn't believe anything about Tripp Shaughnessey's years in the military were the same ole, same ole at all. "You were Special Forces, right?"

He twisted his mouth, a cockeyed smile that answered her plain as day. "What makes you think that?"

It wasn't about anything he'd done. Simply about who he was. "Because I can't see you settling for less than being the center of attention."

"Ah, but that's the thing about Special Ops." He leaned forward, kissed the tip of her nose. "We're not supposed to draw any attention."

"I knew it. I was right."

He conceded nothing. Only cupped her cheek,

rubbed a thumb along her cheekbone. "Does that mean you're going to trust me now?"

"Stay put, you mean."

"It's nothing but semantics, sweetheart. Nothing but that."

Danh paced the length of the service counter, staring at the meats, cheeses, sauces and vegetables though what he saw instead was the disappointment on Mr. Cam's face.

This was a simple operation. He had prepared for all contingencies. Having an off-duty police officer in the shop at the time of his plan's execution should have made no difference at all.

His men were highly trained. The fact that the two assigned to secure the customers hadn't seen the call made to 9-1-1 troubled him. He had failed in their training, and now all six of them were in danger.

The sandwich shop's telephone began ringing. The police making contact, determining his demands, seeing to the state of the hostages. Was anyone hurt? Would he release any women he held? Could they talk to one of the hostages?

Soon the proper authorities would be called and the necessary technical experts gathered to cut off the shop's electricity. Whether this happened before or after negotiators were brought in would be based on Danh's intent to cooperate.

Danh, of course, had no such intent at all.

He would not betray Mr. Cam. He and all his men knew that death was a possibility at any time. Today could as easily be the day as tomorrow.

The ringing of the phone finally ceased. The bullhorn started up again, as did sniffling from the

two women customers who had been dining together. He needed the hostages out of the way and
caught the gaze of one of his men while gesturing
encompassingly. "Take the hostages into the back
hallway."

The sniffling increased and was accompanied
by whimpers. Danh paid no attention until one of
his men ran back into the shop and called, *"O dau,
Qua^n?"*

Danh's head came up sharply, an animal sens-
ing a predator. Qua^n had been posted as lookout.
He would never have left his post willingly. Meaning . . .

Danh headed into the back hallway. He tried
the alley door. It remained locked from the inside.
Both restrooms remained empty. Leaving no other
option but the storeroom locked from the inside.

He shook his head slowly, allowing peace to settle over him. And then he reached for his gun and
fired.

Six

"Fuckin' shit on a stick."

Tripp grabbed Glory by the shoulders, twirled her bodily across the room and into a tight corner where two of the shelving units met at a right angle.

"I know this part," she whispered as he wedged her inside. "Stay put."

He nodded, drew his gun, pressed his back to the wall at her side. The door slammed open, bounced off the cinder blocks behind. Tripp held the weapon raised, both hands at the ready, his heart doing a freight train in his chest.

Beside him, Glory barely breathed. The shelf of supplies to his right blocked his view of the door but didn't keep his nostrils from flaring, his neck hairs from bristling, his adrenaline from pumping like gasoline.

He sensed their visitor long before the black-garbed man swung around and aimed his gun straight at Glory's head. The intruder stepped

over his own downed associate and held out a
gloved hand.

"Give me the gun and she will not die."

Tripp cursed violently under his breath, weighing his options on a different scale than he
would've used in this situation had Glory not been
involved.

If he'd had time to do more than react, time to
think, plot and plan, he would've stashed the gun
behind a can of olives and used the butt end to up
his own prisoner count when the time was right.

Instead, he found himself surrendering the very
piece that would've gone a long way to protecting
Glory from this thug. Now he was stuck using
nothing but the wits that never seemed to operate
at full throttle unless he had a contingency plan.

Right now all he had was a gut full of bile. That
and a big fat regret that he didn't think better on
his feet than he did.

Having passed off the gun, he raised both hands,
palms out. "Let's neither of us go off half-cocked
here."

The other man considered him for a long,
strange moment, his black eyes broadcasting zero
emotion while he stared for what seemed like forever before he tugged the ski mask from his head.

He was young. Tripp would've guessed twenty-
three, twenty-four. Except when he looked at the
kid's eyes. His expression was so dark, so blank, so
unfeeling it was like looking at a long-dead corpse.

Without moving his gaze from Tripp's, the kid
shouted sharp orders in Vietnamese. Two other
similarly garbed goons entered the storeroom and
dragged away the deadweight Tripp had left in the
middle of the floor.

Once the cast of extras was gone, the lead player

planted his feet and shifted his gaze between Tripp and Glory, both hands hanging at his sides, one worrying the ski mask into a black fabric ball, the other flexed and ready and holding the gun.

"An interesting situation we find ourselves in here, isn't it?" he finally asked. "Miss Brighton, would you introduce me to your friend?"

"What do you want?" she asked before Tripp could stop her. "Tell me what you want. I'll give it to you, and you can get out of my shop."

His black hair fell over his brow. "If what I have come for was so easily obtained, then I would have it in my possession by now."

He was after whatever the courier from the diamond exchange had delivered to the Spectra agent. Tripp was sure of it. Was sure as well the information would detail future packets removed from Sierra Leone.

The ski mask fell to the floor. "I'm waiting, Miss Brighton."

"He's a friend. A customer." Her hands fluttered at her waist. "We're just . . . good friends."

"You allow all your customers to visit your storeroom?" His mouth twisted cruelly. "Or only the ones with whom you are intimate?"

Glory gasped. Tripp placed his arm in front of her, a protective barrier he knew did little good. "C'mon, man. There's no need to go there."

The Asian kid raised a brow. "Actually, I think there is. Getting what I want often requires me to explore a defense's most vulnerable link. It is not always pleasant, but it can be quite effective."

Tripp was pissed and rapidly getting more so. "Well, there are no links here to explore. So do as the lady suggested. Take what you've come for and let us all get back to our lives."

"Were it only so simple," he said as he gestured Glory forward. She forced her way past the barricade of Tripp's arm. "But we seem to have hit what will no doubt be an endlessly long impasse thanks to one of Miss Brighton's customers."

Glory looked from the kid back to Tripp, her eyes asking questions to which he had zero answers. "I don't understand."

"You are very predictable, Miss Brighton. As is your customer base. Same sandwiches. Same lunch hours. That made planning this job quite easy. I'm assuming the courier using your place of business for a drop point found your tight schedule advantageous, too."

Tripp's mind raced like the wind. The kid was talking way too much. His gang had blacked out the shop's single security camera, had made entry without alerting anyone to their presence, had secured the scene and done it all while Tripp made love to Glory.

Fuckin' shit on a stick barely covered it. He'd been monitoring the shop for weeks and he'd never noticed the place being scouted. He hadn't been wise to the entire intrusion until the police bullhorn had sounded outside.

A guy who followed through on such flawless planning didn't start yapping his flap unless he felt there would be no survivors but him. And Tripp had a feeling they were looking into the eyes of an animal who'd fight to the death before being taken alive.

"I'm sorry," Glory was saying. Tripp heard the tears in her voice. "I really have no idea what you're talking about or what you want."

She stood in the center of the room where minutes before the downed man had lain. The kid walked in a circle around her, clearly agitated now. An agitation that had sweat gathering in Tripp's armpits.

He didn't like the look that had come into the other man's eyes or the tic twitching in the vein at his temple. It was a look that shimmered with the need for revenge. An ugly need. An ugly revenge.

"Listen," Tripp started, cut off by the kid's sharply spoken, "Do not speak," which was followed by instructions called through the door in his own language. Seconds later, another man appeared and, on orders, approached. "Turn around. Hands behind your back."

Now Tripp was beyond being pissed off. Especially when, at his hesitation, the kid pressed the gun barrel to Glory's head. His palms slick with sweat, Tripp turned and stared blindly at the storeroom's cinder block wall. Blindly, because all he saw was Glory's terrified expression.

That solid reality, her fear, was what he needed to keep forefront in his mind. This wasn't a mission where he had others watching his back. This was a solo run. This was about her life. And he knew she had a lot better chance of coming out of this in one piece with him keeping his head.

The thug at his back bound Tripp's hands together with a zip tie that came close to cutting off his circulation. He bit down hard on his anger and turned around, maintaining as passive an expression as his temper allowed while the kid's henchman patted him down.

Once the third man was gone, Tripp asked, "Now what?"

"Now you tell me your name."

Unless undercover or disguised, all the Smithson operatives existed in the private sector as the engineering project consultants they were. "Shaughnessey."

The kid nodded. "My name is Danh Vuong. I find negotiations so much more effective when personalized. Does that make sense to you Mr. Shaughnessey? Miss Brighton?"

Tripp nodded without agreement, wishing Julian Samms were here. Julian could read people as if they were printed on paper. Tripp had only his instincts to work from.

And those instincts were screaming at him to put this kid down. The way he was pacing and circling Glory. The way his forehead beneath his shock of black hair had beaded with sweat. He was on his way to careening out of control.

Tripp needed to draw the other man's attention away from Glory and onto himself without blowing his civilian cover. "It's tough to negotiate anything when we don't know what it is you want."

"What I want is something Miss Brighton is going to help me get." Vuong looked from Tripp to Glory. Or, more precisely, he looked at Glory's breasts where her chest rose and fell beneath the ribbed knit of her tank top.

The fabric was a pale pink and it hugged her body the way any man liked to see a tight tank top do. Zippers that matched those on her skirt decorated both shoulder straps.

With Tripp looking on, Vuong flipped one of the zipper pulls up and down using his gun barrel's tip.

Glory literally threatened to shake out of her shoes.

"Dude, hey. Would you get the gun out of the lady's face?" Tripp surged forward, purposefully awkward—only to have the Beretta shoved against his Adam's apple until he choked.

He continued to cough and gag as Vuong backed him into the wall. "You, Mr. Shaughnessey, are on the verge of becoming my biggest liability to date. Don't move. Don't speak unless you are spoken to. I would hate to mar this operation by killing you, but I won't hesitate if you give me reason."

Giving the kid reason would mean endangering Glory further. Tripp had yet to meet a killer who had qualms about removing all human roadblocks to his goal.

Once Vuong released him, Tripp dipped his head, working to clear what felt like a permanent constriction in his throat. He watched the kid return to Glory and this time run the gun barrel underneath the curves of both her breasts.

Her nipples tightened, a response to the stimulation that was all about the same fear widening her eyes.

"Very nice." Vuong moved the gun barrel higher, circling one of the taut peaks now pressing through both bra and tank top. "Very nice. Tell me, Mr. Shaughnessey. Does she respond this nicely to your touch? Or is she only turned on by the idea of losing her life?"

Fucking bastard. Talking about Glory as if she didn't exist. Still, Tripp didn't say a word. He'd been spoken to, asked a direct question. It didn't matter. His voice was stuck in his damaged throat, his words battling in his head to be heard.

Vuong turned his gaze in Tripp's direction. "Feel free to answer, Mr. Shaughnessey. In fact, I insist."

Tripp cleared his throat with a grunting sort of cough. "That's fear, man. Not arousal."

Vuong nodded thoughtfully, his eyes waking from the dead. "Our bodies are so complicated, yes? Yours, for example, is as tight as a wenched cable unloading cargo from a ship. While mine is . . . what do you think, Miss Brighton?"

"About what?" she asked softly, her voice steadier than Tripp would have thought.

But that was probably because he was back on the strange idea of a cable unloading a cargo ship. A background piece he filed away.

"About my body language. What emotion am I broadcasting?"

When Glory raised a brow uncertainly, he nodded once. Whatever the intent of the other man's question, Tripp wanted to see Vuong's reaction to Glory's response.

"Uh, I think you might be a bit nervous or upset since things haven't gone the way you were expecting."

Vuong silently considered her words before stepping close enough to drag the gun barrel along the waistband of her skirt. She gasped, trembled. Tripp seethed, steam bellowing from his nostrils, but he stayed where he was.

He needed to get to the knife he'd left with the security equipment after cutting into the coaxial cable. To do that, he needed the bastard out of the room.

But launching himself forward and driving his shoulder into Vuong's gut wasn't the way to get it done.

"She is right, you know, Mr. Shaughnessey." Vuong had obviously sensed Tripp's barely controlled fury since he swung the gun toward him in warning. "At least about me being upset. But then, who wouldn't be after having a plan foiled by an unforeseen circumstance."

"What circumstance?" Glory whispered.

Vuong glanced back at her face before dropping his gaze the length of her body and nuzzling the gun along the zippered fly of her skirt.

"One of your customers. An off-duty police officer managed to dial 9-1-1 on his cell phone and leave the connection open as we were seeing to his safety. Had he simply left well enough alone, we would've been long on our way."

Glory nodded. Tripp waited. Vuong pressed his body into Glory's side and slipped his gun hand beneath her skirt.

"I hate John Waynes," he said as tears rolled silently down her cheeks.

Tripp's gut knotted with the furious boiling of his blood. He twisted his wrists this way and that, shifted a step to the side and fingered the shelving, looking for an edge or protruding bolt sharp enough to saw through his bonds.

"I came to this country when I was ten years old," Vuong was saying. "I naively thought cowboys still roamed the land and rescued innocent victims. I expected justice. But the world is not about justice, is it Miss Brighton?"

Glory looked at Tripp for help, her expression transmitting everything she felt. That if she said anything wrong, the gun beneath her skirt would explode.

He hadn't been spoken to, so not speaking seemed the wisest move. It also seemed like a cowardly one, when everything inside him screamed that he should roar like a lion and deal with the fallout that came.

And so he mouthed the only thing he thought might help. The only words that he knew she'd be able to read from his lips: *I love you.*

The shaky smile at the corner of her mouth bloomed in her eyes. He doubted she believed him, but at least he'd given her hope.

"Justice, Miss Brighton?"

"It should be," she said tentatively. "But, you're right. Too often it's not."

Vuong moved around behind her then and her sigh of relief filled Tripp's lungs. He wasn't even aware he'd forgotten to breathe.

"You're wrong, Miss Brighton. The world is as it should be. It's all about loyalty. Loyalty and suffering."

Glory shook her head. "I don't understand."

Tripp didn't understand either. That didn't stop him from tuning in with his antennae zinging. Or from slowly continuing to rub the zip tie along the edge of the shelving unit that had already drawn his wrist's blood.

"Your customer was loyal to his profession. I admire that. But because of that, he will suffer. I, too, must be loyal to my employer." He stood behind her now and wrapped his arm around her waist.

The arm with the hand still holding the gun. "Even if my loyalty causes suffering as well."

And then he slipped his free hand beneath Glory's skirt and reached between her legs.

Seven

Glory froze. She wanted to bolt, to scream, to spin around and knock the shit out of the man at her back. But he held her too tightly, he had a gun, and Tripp had told her he loved her.

So she froze.

Tripp didn't really love her. What he was doing was keeping her spirits up. Distracting her from the fact that the gangster holding her shop under siege was now feeling up her ass.

Violation was a term she'd never thought of in personal terms. It was more about library fines, ignoring an expiration date when the milk still tasted good. It was about crossing the street on red. About pulling tags off of mattresses.

Now she understood the difference. And she wanted to curl into a fetal position and die.

Only the look on Tripp's face kept her upright. A look that told her this other man's touch wasn't about sex but about control, about power. A brow daring her to defy his certainty that she could handle anything. A set of jaws that ordered her to hold on, to be strong.

She lifted her chin. He nodded his approval. And then she did the unthinkable. She issued her own challenge to the man at her back by spreading her legs.

He released her almost immediately, walked around her as if considering whether to shoot her or slap her down. Before he could do either, the police bullhorn sounded. The shop's phone began to ring. A second later, one of his men called out.

A break in the impasse. She wanted to weep with joy.

"You'll have to excuse me, Miss Brighton. It seems I have business to take care of."

Glory didn't even nod. She simply closed her eyes while he secured her hands behind her as Tripp's were secured. When Danh walked out of the storeroom, he even had the courtesy to close the door.

It wasn't like they could keep him from coming back, considering he'd shot the lock off.

Silence descended. She'd never before realized how nearly soundproof this room really was. All she could hear was her heart beating out *you're alive, you're alive.*

She opened her eyes then and met Tripp's bright gaze, starting forward, wanting to throw her arms around him more than she wanted to breathe.

But all she could do was lean into his body as he leaned into the wall, tuck her face into the cradle of his shoulder, and swear to get her hands on him at the earliest possibility.

"What the hell is happening? Oh, God, I thought I was going to be sick." Even now she feared hyperventilation. "Who is this freak?"

Tripp nuzzled his chin to the top of her head. "I'm not sure, sweetheart. He's a pro, whoever he is."

"This is insane. What could he possibly be looking for here?" She listened to the slight scratch of his midday beard against her hair, to the drumbeat of his heart beneath her cheek.

"I don't think it's about the shop. I think it's about him wanting something someone out there has."

"One of the customers? The cop?" Who had she seen after she'd rang up Wes's order and before she'd come in here to count olives?

The two secretaries from the investment firm on the next block who took a late lunch every day. The professor writing his memoir who always sat near the front window. The off-duty cop she didn't know. The driver for the *Post* who usually came in on Thursdays.

Tripp shook his head. "No. Not the cop."

And how would he know . . . ? She stepped back far enough to look him straight in the eye. "You know who it is, don't you?"

When he didn't respond either to confirm or deny, she pressed harder. "You know who it is the same way you knew someone would see the SOS you tapped out on that cable."

Again with the blankly uncommitted look.

"Dammit, Shaughnessey. You'd better start talking and now."

"You're safer not knowing."

"Safer?" Was he crazy? "Are you out of your mind? I've had a gun to my head, to my chest, and up my skirt. You call that safer?"

"Safer than being dead."

"Who's to say that's not next on our Mr. Vuong's agenda?"

Tripp's silence was answer enough.

"Please, Tripp. If I'm going to die, I'd like to know the reason."

"I'll feel better about telling you once my hands are free."

A weird response. At least it wasn't a no—though once she wiggled her wrists against her own bonds she realized it might as well have been. "Is there a trick to getting out of these things?"

"Yeah." He nodded toward the storage cabinet. "My knife. If I get it down, you think you can cut through this plastic without slicing off my hands?"

"As long as you return the favor."

He grinned at that, buzzed her cheek with a kiss as he headed for the storage cabinet, visually measuring the distance to the shelf where he'd left his knife and coming up short.

Or at least short for a man who wasn't a double-jointed circus act. He only needed another foot at the most . . .

"Here," she said, toeing a gallon can of jalapeño peppers off the bottom of the nearest shelf and sliding it across the concrete floor.

Tripp stepped up, stretched up . . . "Shit. I need another six inches."

"I wouldn't be saying that to just any girl if I were you."

He glared down at her. "Making funnies in the face of death, are we?"

A shiver turned her spine to jelly. "Do you think we're going to die?"

"No, Glory. We're going to live to tell our grandkids about this." He hopped down, glanced around the storeroom.

"Here. Let me try." She was shorter than he was

but knew from watching his attempt that she had a more flexible range of motion.

Unfortunately, she would need five-foot arms to reach. She hopped back down. "Crud. Wait. Shove that crate over."

The plastic box in the room's far back corner held napkins and sandwich bags imprinted with her old logo. Tripp shoved and kicked it into place and climbed up.

The extra height was enough. He grabbed around, his hand smacking the shelf, the wiring, the TV screen, and finally the knife.

He jumped down, scooted the crate back into place while she closed the cabinet doors. He then ordered her to, "Back up. I'll cut you free first."

She did, reaching for his fingers that were warm and reassuring and then suddenly not there. She looked back over her shoulder. Then turned all the way around. "Tripp?"

He was mentally in another time zone, standing there shaking his head. "I'm not so sure."

What! She literally stomped her foot. "Dammit, Shaughnessey. What're you waiting for?"

"For a time when we need the upper hand."

"We need it now!" she wailed.

He shook his head. He'd turned into this robotic machine. Thinking, not feeling. "We'll need it later more than we need it now."

"Later? I don't want to be here later. I want to get out of here now."

The only sound she heard in response was the click as he closed up the knife.

"Tripp," she whined, begged, entreated. "Don't do this to me, please?"

But he ignored her and her pleas, his gaze canvassing the room at hip level as he searched for a place to stash the knife. An easily accessible place for the "later" when he expected to need it.

That place turned out to be an open box of Advil packets she provided for her employees. The lip of the box slanted at enough of an angle to hide the contents. The knife disappeared beneath the plastic squares of white and peacock blue.

Now it was her turn to snag his attention. She approached until she stood full in his face, then approached further, backing him into the wall as she spoke. "If you don't tell me who the hell you are and what the hell is going on, I'll use that knife on you myself."

A grin spread over his mouth, easing the tense lines into which he'd set his jaw. But the tendons in his neck did not relax. And his eyes remained strangely distant.

"You promised," she goaded when still he didn't speak.

"I'm not so sure I promised," he hedged.

"You told me you'd tell me what you thought was going on here. So I wouldn't go to my grave wondering."

"I should've let you cut me free."

"Change of heart?"

"Yeah." He sighed heavily. "I'd really like to hold you."

"Oh, Tripp." The sting of tears threatened to blind her. She pressed herself to him; he was the one solid thing in the room that gave her hope.

"I'm not going to let you go to your grave, Glory." He paused, she waited, the punch line came. "Not till I've gotten mine."

She shook her head. His chest beneath her cheek vibrated with his chuckle when she stuck out her tongue. "Blackmail works both ways, you know."

"That's what I was afraid of. Besides, I was lying. I'm not going to let you die whether I get in your pants again or not. I'm not going to let anything happen to either of us."

The segue was perfect. "You sound pretty confident there for an engineering project consultant."

"Yeah, well, that's the thing. Besides the military background, I have a lot of other, uh, outside training."

Her ears perked up, as did her intuition, which told her this armed forces thing was something Tripp rarely talked about. That he hesitated telling her even now—and wouldn't have if not for this anomalic situation in which they found themselves.

"What sort of training?" she prodded when it became obvious he thought he was done. As if she was going to let him off that easily.

"You think we can sit?" he asked, distracting her again.

"Saving your strength along with the knife?"

"Something like that," he answered and slid down the wall to sit, knees bent and spread.

She settled between, leaning her shoulder into his chest and giving herself the visual advantage of being able to look into his eyes.

She wanted to make sure he didn't try to pull anything over on her. Like some big fat lie of a story to make her feel better, hoping she'd forget that in the next moment they both might die.

Eight

Figuring out how much to say about who he was and what he did had never come easy to Tripp. Keeping the existence of SG-5 off the public radar was essential. Keeping it off all military and law enforcement scopes was paramount.

The Smithson Group righted a lot of wrongs bound up in legal red tape along with others that went largely ignored for a variety of political reasons.

SG-5 wouldn't be able to guarantee many happy endings with Big Brother breathing down its back. But if this siege was indeed Glory's Last Stand, he owed her as much of the truth as he could reasonably share.

So when she prodded him with a softly uttered, "Tripp?" he shrugged, and said, "It's no big deal really."

And then she butted him with her shoulder. "You are so full of crap."

A firecracker. A pistol. She was one of a kind and made it really hard for him not to smile. "Now, what makes you say that? You have your own train-ing to compare what's a big deal and what isn't?"

"No, but if you're relying on basic stuff, then Brighton's is a kosher deli."

She wasn't going to let him bullshit his way out of anything, was she, perceptive little wench. "Hmm. I do seem to recall a lot of ham being or-dered up on sandwiches."

"Exactly." She butted him again, but this time she settled close, rubbing her cheek against his chest when she was done. "You're thinking on your feet. You're making decisions on the fly, using familiar skills, not ones stored in your memory banks."

"Hmm," he mused again because humming was easier than burying the truth beneath a smooth bundle of lies—lies she'd never believe anyway.

He swore then and there that no other woman had ever seen him so clearly. And then he swore for being way too pleased that she did.

So when she said, "Tripp?" in a voice that was all sugar and spice, one he knew would be matched by a dreamy soft look in her doe-bright eyes, he couldn't help it. He gave in and looked down.

And she either wasn't as frightened as she'd been claiming to be or she really thought he could save her.

Tripp sighed. It was bloody damned hell having a woman look at you like that. Like you were the hero she'd been waiting for.

He pretended that he needed to clear his throat. "Thing is, Glory, I'm not exactly an engi-neering project consultant."

She nodded with way too much know-it-all en-thusiasm—which made her *such* an easy target to tease.

"I leap tall buildings in single bounds. I spin

webs in any size. You know," he added, struggling
to keep a straight face. "To catch thieves. Like they
were flies."

"Dammit, Shaughnessey. I'm going to have to
hurt you now."

He braced himself for the attack, nose scrunched,
eyes screwed up. So he was totally unprepared for
her to kiss him. And that was exactly what she did.

Her lips moved lightly over his, trembling as she
murmured his name, and plea after plea to help
her, to talk to her, to tell her that they'd both be
okay.

He didn't have the use of his hands, goddamn
it, and could only shift around until he was sitting
sideways and could press her skull to the wall.

He silenced her murmurs with a bruising, pun-
ishing kiss. She had no idea what she was asking
How he had sworn never to make promises to anyone again.

But she tasted like fine spun cotton candy, like
all the good things a man wanted in his life. And
he knew that long-ago oath wasn't worth the air
he'd written it on that first night spent on his belly
crawling through Colombia's rain forest with co-
caine on his fingertips and a bullet in his thigh.

He kissed her anyway, because it was better than
thinking, than talking, and because she just plain
knew how to kiss. So few women did, or even knew
what a kiss did to a man. How nothing but the feel
of soft lips and compliance could bring him to his
knees.

Glory's kiss did it all, which was why he had to
pull away, ease away, set her away and give her the
truth. "I trained in Special Ops and spent more
than a few years as a sniper."

"A sniper?" she asked, her voice low and awed. "Like with a gun?"

"No," he replied, wanting none of her awe. "With my dick."

She glared deeply into his eyes. "You, Shaughnessey, are cruisin' for a bruisin'."

"Maybe so," he admitted, lightening up the mood. "But at least I'm cruisin' faster than a speeding bullet."

She silently studied his face for a moment before she asked, "Have you killed people?"

He nodded, added, "No one who didn't deserve it."

"You're comfortable making that call?"

He'd had to be. It was kill or be killed. Kill or watch innocent victims die of bullets, of abuse, needles in their veins or powder up their nose. "Are you going to judge me now? Change your mind about dessert?"

She rocked her head side to side. "I think all I'm doing is trying to figure you out."

"That could take a fairly long lifetime. I haven't yet managed it and I've been living with myself for, uh, quite a few years."

"How many?" she asked and nearly caught him off guard.

He leaned forward, rubbed his nose over hers. "Now, sweetheart. Numbers don't matter. You're only as old as you feel."

"Since my hands aren't free at the moment to do any feeling, I need you to tell me."

"You are a clever little thing, aren't you."

"Actually, this faux cleverness is a weak attempt to keep my mind occupied." She sighed, deflated, closed her eyes for a moment, then opened them and stared across the room. "Otherwise, I'm going to think too much about what's going to happen next and whether I'm going to walk out of here alive."

"You will. We both will."

"How do you know?"

"It's what I do, remember? All that web-spinning and building-leaping?" When she looked even less convinced, he sighed. "Glory, listen to me. Even if the SOS wasn't picked up, I'll get us out of here. This is what I do. I need you to trust me."

"I do. It's just . . ."

"Just what?"

"It's just that I had an argument with my mother this morning and we didn't exactly hang up the phone on the best of terms."

God, but she was going to break his heart. Yet he went on making promises anyway. "No worries. You two can kiss and make up as soon as we're out of here."

"Do you think she and my father know what's happening?"

"With the police out front? I'm sure NewsChannel 4 is already on the scene. Plus, wanting to learn what they could about the shop . . ."

"The cops would've called my parents." She dropped her gaze, shifted so that she was leaning more against the wall than against him. "I don't want them to worry. I wish I could let them know I'm okay."

He hated that he couldn't offer her the cell phone he'd taken off the lookout. But Vuong could return any second and Tripp wasn't about to give up any advantage.

"Right now it's a standoff. No shots have been fired and no demands made."

"That we know of, anyway."

He nodded. "True. But this Danh Vuong didn't sound like a man with demands to make of anyone outside. What he wants is in here."

"That's what I don't get. I don't launder money or harbor political prisoners. What could he possibly want?"

Tripp blew out a long breath. If he told her the truth, he'd be jeopardizing his own case by exposing the Spectra agent. But he'd also have an intelligent and informed ally. And that never hurt in a pinch.

He bit the bullet. "The professor working on his memoir is not a professor. He's an agent of an international crime syndicate and he's using your shop as a drop point."

"A drop point," she echoed.

"A courier from Marian Diamonds is either being blackmailed into giving up details on illegal shipments out of Sierra Leone or is selling his soul to the devil."

"And you know this how? No, wait." She closed her eyes, shook her head. "I'm dizzy with these webs you're spinning, Tripp."

"Sorry, sweetheart. It's not a pretty life I lead. But I figure it's best you realize what you're dealing with here."

"What I'm dealing with? Are you kidding? I can't digest half of what you've said. Well, except for the part where you swore you wouldn't let anything happen to me."

"Did I say that?"

"I sure hope I didn't dream it. Though, actually, if I were dreaming all of this it would be a whole lot easier to deal with because morning would be on the way." She settled closer again. "You know, morning? Waking up? Stretching, yawning, getting a cup of coffee?"

"What about the smooching?"

One dark brow went up. "Smooching?"

"Smooching, cuddling. All those juicy early morning wake-up goodies."

"And here I thought you were above all that physical stuff."

"Are you kidding? That physical stuff is what guys are made off."

"What happened to frogs and snails and puppy dog tails?"

"Ah, those were the days."

"Right. Now it's all about spiderwebs," she said and collapsed in on herself as if she'd exhausted her energy reserve.

Tripp had to keep her going. She'd be better able to stand up to Vuong, stay safe, stay strong, when alert. "What were you and your mother arguing about?"

Her eyes fluttered open and she laughed with a reckless hysteria. "About my choices in men."

"Oh, really." He perked up at that. "Sounds like a better way to pass the time than talking about me."

"What makes you think talking about the men in my life doesn't include you?"

"Does it?" he asked with a gulp.

"It should. Especially considering my mother's biggest complaint is that my two longest-running relationships have been with men belonging to a questionably criminal element."

"I'm crushed. Criminal element indeed."

She shrugged. "Hey, if the web fits."

He chuckled. "Funny girl."

"Do you have one, Tripp?"

"A web? A criminal element?"

"A girl."

He sighed, leaned forward to nuzzle his nose against her temple, breathing in the sweet smell of her hair. "I'm pretty sure I do. At least I'm working on it."

"Oh, Tripp." She dusted kisses over his cheek, huddling up into the cradle of his neck and shoulder. "When we get out of here, can we work a little harder? Together? I'd really like it if we could."

"You're not just saying that because you want to swing on my web, are you?"

"No, I'm saying it because you've teased me for months. And because I didn't get the chance earlier to finish what I started."

He pretended to ponder. "That's true. That was all rather one-sided."

"Not my intention, trust me."

Talking about sex here and now seemed a bit like fiddling while the *Titanic* went down. But he was up for any distraction to keep Glory calm.

It was unfortunate Vuong had bound their hands. And damn unfortunate that Tripp himself had been the one to stash the knife.

"Well, if your intentions involve giving as good as you got, I'm all for some heavy-duty exploration of what you have on your mind."

"Giving as good as I got? You think rather highly of yourself, don't you Shaughnessey?"

"I'm just a man confident in his skills."

"Oh, I see," she said, her mouth twisting around what he was sure was a hell of a laugh at his expense. "What're you going to do if I give even better?"

"Guess I'll be up a creek and have to do a lot of extra paddling to make up for it."

"If by paddling you mean spanking, no thanks. But if by paddling you mean, well . . ."

Cute. She'd embarrassed herself into a corner. He leaned forward and kissed her on the lips, rubbing his lips over hers lightly, gently, teasingly, because he wanted her to be the one to open up and beg.

He wanted that because it was so much easier to let himself fall when he knew he wasn't falling alone.

When she opened her mouth, she opened it with a whimpering groan, bathing his lips with the barest tip of her tongue before pressing the seam where he held his mouth in a tightly determined line.

The funny thing about determination, he mused, was how quickly the reasoning behind it fell into a big black hole of need. The physical, he readily owned up to. The emotional, however, he was just beginning to understand when the storeroom door crashed open for the second time.

Nine

Glory jerked away from the bliss that was Tripp and banged the back of her head on the wall. Tripp scrambled to his feet. She wasn't quite as quick, what with not being a superhero and wearing a really short skirt.

Boy, it had seemed like a good idea at the time she'd been dressing this morning. And, boy, what she wouldn't give to turn back the clock and start this day over. She'd wear a flour sack and a chastity belt if given the magical chance.

But this was her reality, and she managed to stand just as the professor who wasn't came stumbling into the storeroom, Danh shoving him from behind.

Danh looked from Tripp to Glory to the older man who had gained his balance and now stood in the center of the room. Danh circled the professor or the agent or whoever the hell the man was, prodding him with the business end of his gun.

"Here are the rules for this party. Mr. Shaughnessey, you will sit back down."

Glory glanced at Tripp's inscrutable expression, watching his gaze never waver from Danh's, watching as he slid down the wall to sit.

"Very well done," Danh said, turning his attention to her. "Miss Brighton, you will turn around so I can cut you free."

Her heart fluttered at the thought of gaining her freedom, sank at the realization that she wasn't free at all. Simply being used as a pawn in Danh's game.

Facing Tripp, she presented Danh with her bound hands, wincing as he cut through the hard plastic tie. Blood rushed back into her wrists and fingers; she clasped her hands at her waist and rubbed at the bruises.

Tripp's face remained impossible to read. She had no idea if he wanted her to play nice, make a run for the door, maybe try to slip his knife out of the Advil box and use it.

Or, if all she needed to do was distract Danh by cooperating with whatever he had in mind while Tripp did what he had been trained to do.

In the end, the decision was taken out of her hands when Danh gave her a directive. "Now, Miss Brighton. I'm going to have you search the professor here for the information he has that belongs to my employer."

Knowing the man wasn't a professor at all but a member of a crime syndicate should've made the prospect easier to face. But, in fact, the opposite was true.

She looked up at his kindly, forgiving expression and tried to smile in return. Knowing the evil heart that beat beneath his tweed jacket and chocolate cashmere turtleneck sent her thoughts racing in directions she didn't want them to go.

The idea of the crimes he might have committed, the horrors he'd perpetrated . . . she couldn't even pry her fingers apart to touch his clothes.

"Haven't you done that already? Searched him, I mean?"

"Cursorily. I want you to be more thorough. One hundred percent thorough. And you can start by helping him remove his jacket."

Glory moved around behind the professor and lifted shaking hands to his shoulders.

"I'm so sorry about this," she whispered, speaking to the man she wished he was, speaking to herself. Even speaking to Tripp, apologizing for not knowing anything to do to help him get them out of here.

"Don't worry about it, my dear. We are all forced to deal with certain unpleasantries in our lives," he said, shrugging out of fashionable and expensive tweed.

Glory stepped back, holding the jacket by the padded shoulders, waiting for further instruction. The professor smoothed down the rumpled sleeves of his shirt.

Danh moved to face him, his gun now seeming to be an extension of his arm rather than a weapon. "Unpleasantries. An interesting turn of phrase for a man in your profession, yes?"

The professor's gray eyes studied Danh from behind wire-rimmed glasses. "I suppose were you to poll my students, they might agree."

Danh laughed at that, a tight humorless sound that left a trail as it crawled over Glory's skin "We're among friends here. Or at least among those similarly invested in leaving here unexposed."

Glory slid her gaze to Tripp's face. His eyes

were focused on the professor's. And she swore she saw him give the other man a signal. All this subterfuge . . . who did he think she was that she was going to fall apart while these three cats batted around a mouse she couldn't see?

"Miss Brighton. The coat seams, collar, pockets, lining. Shred the garment if you must."

"What am I looking for?"

"Anything that doesn't belong."

"And if I don't find anything?" she asked, fingering the collar from point to point.

"Shoes or shirt next. We strip the professor bare if need be. And then we search his person."

"Wait the hell a minute. I am not taking off this man's clothes."

No sooner had she gotten the words out than she found Danh standing over Tripp and lining up his head as a target. "I think you'll do what you're instructed to do. There will be consequences if you do not."

Tears welled and burned until her vision was nothing but a blur of tweed. That blur was so much better, however, than picturing what a bullet would do to Tripp's head.

She moved to the pockets, the lapels, laying the jacket out on the floor and running her fingers over every inch of the lining as well as the heavier outer fabric. She finally stood, folding it over her arms.

She shook her head. "There's nothing here."

"Professor? Where would you like her to continue?"

"Miss Brighton," the professor addressed her directly. "I understand your concern, but please realize I am aware that you have no choice."

And you? she wanted to ask. If you're who Tripp says you are, what sort of choices do you have? "It would go easier on all of us if you could give me a hint? Or maybe just give Mr. Vuong what he's looking for, and save all of us this hassle?"

"She has a point," Tripp finally put in, Danh having removed the gun from the top of his head. "Give up the goods and we can all go home."

The professor's expression remained unaffected. Apparently he wasn't as put off by having her strip him as she was by the reality of the act. He slipped off his turtleneck with a nonchalance that was strangely disturbing and handed her the shirt.

Danh circled the both of them while she went through the same process of searching seams and hems. "Professor. Why don't you tell us about the memoir you're writing. With your experience, you must have more than a few tales to tell."

Why the hell was Danh baiting the man? Nothing good was going to come of this, Glory just knew. She found nothing embedded anywhere in the shirt and glanced helplessly at Tripp. His response was no more than a look that encouraged her to hang in and he'd figure a way out of here soon.

"I'm not so sure this is the time and place for stories," the professor argued as he heel-toed off both shoes for Glory's inspection.

"It's time for whatever I decide. Do you have a publisher for your memoir? Do you have an audience waiting to read about your life?"

The professor's smile was a picture of paternal patience. "I'm not seeking publication, Mr. Vuong. I'm recording my memories as a self-indulgent exercise more than anything."

"Is that right? So if I have one of my men bring in your portfolio, then you will read to us?"

Glory sensed a shift in the room's tension even before she got to her feet with the shoes hooked over two of her fingers. Tripp had moved from leaning against the wall, his knees drawn up, his hands at his back, to a sitting sort of crouch as if ready to launch himself forward.

The professor, now bare-chested and bare-footed, pushed his glasses farther up his nose. It seemed to Glory that he was using the motion as a cover, or else as a signal to Tripp.

She had no idea what was going on, what part in this drama she was supposed to be playing. So she simply offered Danh the shoes. "There's nothing here."

Danh never even looked at her. He gave all of his attention to the professor, gesturing the length of the other man's body with his gun. "It's your choice, Professor. Hand Miss Brighton your belt and your trousers. Or tell me what you've done with the information passed to you by the courier."

"Courier? I'm sure I don't know what it is you're talking about."

Danh swung. The gun cracked into the professor's skull above his ear. His glasses skidded across the floor and between Tripp's feet. Nobody moved. Glory watched blood trickle between the professor's fingers where he held his hand to his head.

Screw the little punk with the gun. Even if the professor was the agent Tripp said he was, the man didn't deserve this inhumane treatment.

She crossed the room and had her hand on the lid of the plastic storage crate when Danh ordered, "Stop where you are, Miss Brighton."

She mentally flipped him off, opened the crate and gathered a handful of napkins. "I will not stop. This man is bleeding."

She handed the napkins to the professor, then crossed her arms and faced Danh directly. "I'm done here. You obviously don't expect to find any-thing in his clothing. You're just playing some sick game, and it's got to stop."

Even as she said it, she sensed the professor re-moving his belt on her right, Tripp pushing up to his feet on her left. She was in deep shit, she knew it, and she no longer cared. If this was going to be her end, so be it. She just wanted this ridiculous siege of her property over with.

And then Danh began to laugh, a chuckle that was part desperation, part admiration, and a lot of disbelief. When he finally spoke, it was to call out in his language for one of his henchmen, to whom he issued orders while never breaking eye contact with her.

She ignored the professor's offering of the belt, turned to Tripp for help and mouthed, *What now?*

He cast a brief glance toward the professor, gave an even briefer nod before looking at her again and answering with a silent, *Bathroom.*

He wanted her to go to the bathroom. He wanted her out of here. She could only imagine that he had a plan and was sending her out of harm's way. She longed to go, felt she should stay. After all, she was on a roll, albeit a reckless one.

She inhaled deeply, exhaled, and hurried for-ward before she lost her nerve. "Mr. Vuong," was all she got out before his man had taken hold of her upper arm and started propelling her toward the door.

"What's going on? What are you doing?"

"I think you need to freshen up, Miss Brighton, and leave the business of negotiation to the men."

And that was all she heard.

Seconds later, she found herself being shoved through the door and into the women's restroom.

Ten

Glory gripped the edges of the white porcelain sink and hung her head. A part of her wanted to do nothing but break down and sob. Another part of her wasn't sure she'd ever be able to cry again, or if she'd ever have reason to.

If she couldn't come to real tears over *this,* the most horrific experience of her twenty-seven years . . .

Her eyes stung. It was impossible to blink. But still there was nothing. No reaction. Just nothing. Here she was alone, momentarily safe, yet none of the tears that had welled before would come.

She supposed the mind-racing processes of logic and reasoning had squashed all emotional response. And then she snorted. At least some effort could've been put in to answering her number one burning question.

Who the hell *was* Tripp Shaughnessey?

She'd only begun to ponder all the possibilities when she heard a quiet scratching against the ceiling tiles overhead. She brought her gaze up slowly, remained absolutely still but for her eyes that searched the mirror's reflection of the small room behind.

A ceiling tile shifted, dislodged from the frame. A second followed until there was a gaping black hole in the corner nearest the door. She froze, this time not even moving her eyes, staring as a face smeared with camouflage paint appeared in the opening.

Her heart thundered. She tried to swallow her fear but choked. Her palms grew slick with sweat against the cool porcelain sink.

The man put a silencing finger to his lips and she nodded, watching mesmerized as he vanished, then reappeared feet first, dropping to the floor behind her.

She turned around as a second man followed, indistinguishable from the first in the same camo gear. He remained silent and still as a third man appeared.

This one had black hair pulled to his nape in a ponytail. He also seemed to be in charge as he was the only one who spoke. "Are you all right?"

She nodded.

"Is anyone hurt?"

She shook her head.

He pressed his lips together as if satisfied, then asked, "Where's Tripp?"

"In the storeroom," she whispered, her biggest question answered. As if there had really been any doubt. Tripp Shaughnessey was not at all who he seemed.

"We counted six intruders. Is that right?"

She thought for a minute. "It's hard to say. I can't tell one from the next. Except for Danh and the one Tripp knocked out, they're all still wearing their masks. I haven't seen but four together at a time."

"Danh?"

"The one in charge." She swallowed. Her hands began to shake. "The one holding Tripp."

The dark-haired man nodded, turned to his friends, gestured in what looked like a series of coded signals. Both gave sharp affirmative nods of their heads, and then the first man approached.

"I need you to follow my instructions, okay?"

As if she'd expected otherwise. "Sure."

"Lock yourself in one of the stalls and don't move until we're back."

"And if you don't come back?" she asked, because she couldn't help consider the possibility after the day she'd had.

He smiled at that. Camo paint or not, it was a look she was certain had left more than a few women speechless, a look that was all about confidence and certainty, even while it glinted with a cockiness that said she had no idea who she was dealing with.

Before today, she would've agreed. But that was before today. "Right. You'll be back. And what then?"

"First things first," he said and motioned for her to lock herself away.

She did, only reluctantly because she wanted to see and hear and know what was going on. This was her shop, dammit. Her customers, her employee, her livelihood under siege. As it was, she wasn't even able to pace. The space between the toilet and stall door was nil.

She knew Tripp's three associates had left the room, though she'd never heard them go. Now all she could do was wait. She did so with her head braced against the stall door, her body flat, her hands splayed at her sides, her fingers spread. It was a silly pose, really, but it enabled her to breathe calmly instead of hyperventilate.

A thud in the hallway outside brought her head up a short time later. She laced her fingers tightly, then loosely, worrying them at her waist. Minutes passed, or seconds—she had lost all sense of time—another thud sounded, followed by a scuffle, though she never heard a single voice cry out or call orders.

She was crazy with wanting to know what was happening, insane with the realization that there was nothing she could do to help. She was locked in a toilet; it felt so wrong to pray, though she was certain her mother's First Presbyterian prayer circle would tell her a toilet was as good as any place.

And so she did, sending up wishes and hopes and supplications as best she knew how, wondering if any of the unanswered phone calls had been her father checking in, ready to give her his lecture, wondering how hurt her parents would be to know she'd fallen for another dangerous man.

Suddenly she wanted more than anything to ask about her father's meat loaf sandwich. To find out if the potato pancakes had been too salty as they usually were. She wanted to talk to her mother, to hear her scolding voice and promise to go out with any guy she wanted her to meet.

A patently untrue promise, of course, because the only man she wanted in her life was three doors away if she counted the one on the stall. Three doors and an entire lifetime of experience. The fact that he had any interest in her at all left her surprised.

She was no one but Glory Brighton, hardly interesting to a man who had seen the world, though she had to admit she did seem to attract ones followed by trouble. Yet even as she entertained the thought, she knew it wasn't true. Tripp was nothing like the troublemakers she'd known in the past.

He was all about solving problems and saving the world from men like those others. From men like the ones who had threatened all that she knew, all that she had. If she got out of here in one piece, she swore she'd pull a Scarlett O'Hara and take an oath to stand up for what was hers and to never go hungry again.

In the next moment, the bathroom door squeaked open. She spun around, pressed one eye to the crack below the stall's hinges. One by one, the three men returned. Tripp followed. She couldn't stay put any longer and slid back the flimsy lock on the door.

The moment he spread wide his arms, she was there, her face buried against his chest, her arms around his waist, his around hers. He smelled so good. He felt like her world, like he was everything she would ever want or need, and she wasn't sure she knew how to let him go. Knew as well that, for now, she had to.

"Sweetheart, are you okay?" he murmured into her hair.

"What about you?" She pulled away frowning, holding his hands and rubbing the dried blood from the skin on his wrists.

"All in a day's work."

"Your day maybe. Not mine." And upon saying that, the tears finally came. Tears of relief and exhaustion and joy that she would never go hungry again—and that Tripp would be around for her to snuggle with and argue with and make love with another day.

"I've got to go," he said with no small measure of regret. "But I'll be back for you when this is all done."

"What do I do now?" she asked as the phone again started to ring.

"You answer that and tell them you're opening the door."

"And what do I say about"—she glanced toward the hallway where through the door still propped open she saw . . . —"the bodies."

"That a man of steel spun a sticky web." He said it with a smile she wanted to return but couldn't. Not even after he lowered his head, rubbed his nose over the tip of hers, and kissed her soundly.

When he finally lifted his head, she blinked stupidly. His grin cleared her sensual fog. "No, really. What do I say?"

Tripp glanced up as his three associates vanished into the ceiling. He quickly spelled out her cover story. She absorbed it all, ran the explanation over in her mind until she was certain she had no questions.

Then she backed across the room and watched Tripp pull himself up through the gaping hole in the ceiling, disappearing behind the tiles he settled back into place.

Okay. First step. Take a deep breath. Second step. Answer the phone. A move that required she leave the restroom and circumvent the pile of bodies. She could do this. She could do this.

Eyes scrunched up, she scurried down the hallway and into the shop.

"Glory, sheesh." Neal struggled to gain his feet. "Where have you been? What's going on? How'd you get by that son of a bitch?"

"I've got to get the phone, Neal. But come here. I'll cut you loose and you can free the others."

"They're gone?" asked the lighter-haired of the two secretaries, duct tape hanging loose from her mouth. "What happened?"

"Long story made short, they've been put out of commission." Glory said, instead of blurting out the truth of men of steel and webs.

She made but the briefest eye contact with the professor as he entered the room under his own steam to a round of gasps and questions, before she picked up the phone.

"Glory Brighton here."

Tripp showered and changed clothes in the ops center's locker room after an hour spent between the treadmill and the weights.

Julian, Christian and Kelly John had cleaned up first. They had more to clean up, what with the grease paint they'd worn to avoid recognition— the sort of disguise they rarely had to wear.

But they'd been operating on their own turf, in close proximity to the very building housing the office that was their cover. The camouflage had been about self-preservation, not about blending into the jungle of the city.

All any of them could do now was keep their fingers crossed that the strategy had worked.

Wearing nothing but a towel around his waist and another draped over his head, Tripp padded into the dressing area. Glory should be done with the police by now. At least with anything they were going to need her for tonight.

Now it was his turn to get to her and finish what they'd started. He wanted to make sure she was okay, that she wasn't alone and frightened, that she knew he hadn't lied when he'd promised to come back.

He tugged the towel from his head to find he had company. Hank Smithson stood with his hands in his pockets and the butt end of a cigar in the corner of his mouth.

"Julian's off to Miami, but I'm taking Christian and Kelly John to dinner since they're pissin' and moanin' about never gettin' their lunch." Hank rocked back on his boot heels. "You up for a steak?"

Lunch, right. The reason he'd gone to Brighton's all those hours before. Tripp pulled his duffel out of his locker, tossed his towel to the bench behind him.

"Actually, I'm off to see a girl about a promise," he said, stepping into his boxers.

Hank nodded, shifted his cigar to the other side of his mouth. "I figured you might be thinking of something along those lines. Kinda surprised to hear you've been making promises, though."

Buttoning the fly on his jeans, Tripp glanced over with a grin. "Yeah, sorta shocked myself with that one."

"The girl's a good influence."

"She gets my jokes," Tripp said, surprising himself. "She doesn't necessarily laugh, but she gets them."

Hank stopped rocking, pulled his hands from his pockets and crossed his arms over his chest. "Maybe she knows what I know. That life doesn't have to be funny all the time. That doesn't mean it ain't worth living."

Tripp tugged a black T-shirt down over his head, sat to pull on socks and his boots. "Guess I'm pretty transparent, huh?"

"No. You just need to forgive yourself for the things no one else holds against you. The past is the past, son. You need to see to your future."

"With Glory, you mean?"

Hank turned to go. "With whoever makes you happy for all the right reasons."

Ten minutes later, Tripp stood on the sidewalk, arms crossed, hands in his pits, watching the lights of the ambulances and patrol cars flash off Brighton's front glass.

The hostages had been examined by paramedics, statements had been taken by detectives, and the scene combed by the forensics team. The media was now out in force.

He figured the patrol cars in the distance were hauling Vuong's gang away, finishing the job the SG-5 team had started. Good riddance to the lot of the bastards for the scare they'd given Glory.

A scare Tripp still felt burning like an ember he'd stepped on with bare feet. Damn, but he'd come way too close to losing her and any chance to tell her how crazy he was with wanting to get to know her.

A new burst of cameras flashing had him looking toward the door just as Glory came out flanked by two people he'd bet money were her parents. Her mother even had the same curly head of hair. A policeman in front of them staved off reporters as the three slid into the back of his car.

Good. She was on her way home with an escort who would make sure she got there. Relief swept through him; he'd had no idea he was still so tense. Or so hungry to see her again. He'd give them time, hang out for a while until they'd finished up their reunion. Then he'd make his move.

It was when he stepped back and turned to go that his world fell apart. In the crowd across the street he saw one face staring his way.

Danh Vuong.

Sonofabitch.

He must've escaped during the melee of the cops separating victims from violators. Through the alley door, most likely, though Tripp couldn't believe that entrance wouldn't have been under surveillance all afternoon.

But how he'd gotten loose from the ropes . . . double-jointed little fuck, dislocating his own shoulder while Tripp looked on, demonstrating exactly how he'd slipped his hands free.

Tripp stood immobile, watching the Asian kid, torn between charging across the street or grabbing the closest cop, knowing he could do neither without jeopardizing SG-5.

He'd have to explain how he knew Vuong. What he'd seen. How he'd gotten free. Why he'd left all the others behind. Who the Spectra agent was and why his help had been enlisted.

As far as anyone but Glory and the agent knew, Tripp hadn't been there. He couldn't be found out. Couldn't risk exposing SG-5. Couldn't let the others go down because of his mistake.

All he could do was watch Danh Vuong disappear into the crowd.

Eleven

"Mom, I swear I'm fine," Glory said, pulling open her efficiency's front door, having assured her parents of the very same thing for the last hour over hot tea and chicken noodle soup. "All I want to do is soak in the tub for an hour and then sleep for at least twelve."

Ann Brighton stepped into the hallway, both hands tightly gripping the gold chain handle of her tiny black purse. Her curly black hair, so similar to Glory's, was threaded with the silver strands of her age. "I wish you'd reconsider and stay at the house with us. You could go to prayer circle with me in the morning."

Glory wasn't at all opposed to the idea considering today she'd used up her stored allotment of appeals to all higher powers. But right now the only place she wanted to be was in her own bed. "I'll come with you next week, okay?"

Her mother nodded, backed further into the walk-up's tiny hallway, her lips pressed tightly together as if clamping down on further concern.

Milt Brighton followed, giving his daughter a huge hug from which Glory hated to be released. She held tight to his hand until he was out of her reach.

"Your mother's right," he said, pushing his big blocky glasses back into place, running a hand back over his shock of white hair. "We'd both feel better if you'd stay with us."

"I'll lock up tight. I've set the alarm on the windows." She shifted her weight to her other hip, cocked her head. "Besides, the break-in had nothing to do with me, and the perpetrators are locked up. I'll be fine."

"Promise you'll call if you need anything. If you just want to talk. If you want us to come back." Her mother glanced over Glory's shoulder into the apartment's main room. "We could stay now, sleep on your sofa bed."

"Mom, I'm twenty-seven years old and I've been living on my own for ten of those. I love you to death but I need to unwind here on my own."

Her dad wrapped his arm around her mother's shoulders. "You hear so much as a squeak, you call us, Glory Marie."

"I will, Dad. I promise." She kissed them both once more, then locked up and headed for the bathroom.

Ten minutes later, however, she heard a knock at her door. With her bathwater running and her feet already wet, she slipped into her robe and padded silently through the apartment.

She doubted her parents had returned, but she did not want to face curious neighbors or the insistent media. The eyes she saw, however, when she pressed one of hers to her peephole, were the only eyes she wanted to see.

Her pulse raced in a pitter-patter rhythm. Her palms grew wet enough that she wondered if she'd even be able to unlock and open the door.

Tripp knocked again, more softly this time as if he had decided she was sleeping, didn't want to wake her, was thinking of turning away . . .

She used the pocket of her bathrobe as a hand towel and managed to flip dead bolts, slide locks, and pull open the door before he'd gotten but six feet down the hall.

"Hi," she said breathlessly.

"Hi," he said, sounding winded.

"You look good for a man who's been busy saving the world," she said, her gaze taking in all of him.

He glanced down as if trying to see what she saw. "Part of the job description. Looking good inspires confidence."

"Oh. Is that it?" she asked, and he nodded.

In the quiet that followed, she heard water running. She gestured over her shoulder toward the small bathroom accessible only through her bedroom. "I was about to take a bath and need to get that before I flood my neighbor downstairs. Would you like to come in and wait?"

He stood leaning forward a bit, his hands gripping the door frame as he filled the entrance. The tense set of his jaw told her he had a lot more on his mind than checking up to see that she'd arrived home safely.

And that was okay because her thoughts of him weren't exactly about seeing to his health and well-being. "Tripp?"

His gaze narrowed in on hers. "Get the water. I'll lock the door."

She nodded but barely, because doing more

than breathing suddenly seemed beyond her range of motion. Tripp Shaughnessey was in her apartment behind locked doors.

Dreams really did come true!

She scurried to the bathroom and turned off the water seconds before more than two splats of foamy white bubbles escaped the lip of the clawfoot tub and hit the floor. She slipped one arm from its sleeve, reached down to pull the plug.

She was stopped by Tripp at her back saying, "Don't."

She straightened, turned. "Don't?"

"Don't drain it. Take your bath. I'll wait."

"Okay. The place is small. You should be able to find your way back through." What a stupid thing to say when he'd found his way this far just fine.

"I thought about waiting in here."

Oh. Oh, oh. "You want to watch me bathe?"

He shrugged. "Or bathe you."

"Bathe me?" Oh. Oh, my. "Not bathe with me?"

"I showered while you were finishing up with the police," he said.

It was a hedge, not an answer. That was okay. She was nervous, too. "I saw you, you know."

"When?" he asked, his eyes sparking.

"You were on the sidewalk. When I was leaving with my parents. I thought about waving you over, but realized there would be too many explanations about me knowing you and everything."

She waited for his response, saw a multitude of ones that remained unspoken come and go in his eyes. He finally settled on looking at her with what felt like admiration, like approval, like all the things she wanted him to feel.

And then he reached back and closed the bathroom door.

"I knew there was more to you than this fabulous body," he said, reaching for the collar of her bathrobe and pushing it back, exposing her bare shoulders.

She felt the strange urge to shrug back into the warm chenille, an urge followed quickly by a polar desire to shrug it off completely.

This was what she wanted, wasn't it? To have Tripp all to herself? To explore what might be the relationship she'd been waiting for all of her life?

She let the robe fall and stood wearing fuzzy, red slouch socks, her bra and baggy sleeping boxers.

Tripp's grin spread ear to ear. "Oh, Glory. You are the most amazing woman."

Now she really wanted to grab her bathrobe off the floor and use it to cover all her imperfections and insecurities. There was nothing much amazing about her at all.

He, on the other hand . . .

He was gorgeous beyond belief. And he was looking at her as if she was truly more than he'd expected to see, to find, to discover.

The grin on his face had her nervously rubbing the toes of one sock over the Achilles' tendon of the other. And how apropos considering she was certain he would quickly become her biggest weakness.

When she took a deep shuddering breath, he stepped closer and wrapped one arm around her neck to pull her near.

She buried her face in the crook of his shoulder, absorbing his comforting warmth the way she'd so wanted to do when they'd been held captive.

He nuzzled her ear, her jaw, her throat, whispering soft nonsense about how good she smelled, how soft she was, how beautiful . . . Oh, but this felt so right. And he smelled so crisp and so clean, like a sweet apple tart.

It was when he reached back with his free hand and released the clasp of her bra that she realized they were going to go where she'd wanted to go forever. The straps slipped from her shoulders; she shifted one way then the other until the seamless white cotton fell to the floor.

Tripp set her away then, held her shoulders and her gaze for a long, tense cherry bubble bath–scented moment before he looked down.

Her nipples tightened; she drew back her shoulders, sucked in her stomach, watched his appreciative expression darken seconds before he turned them both around.

He sat on the edge of the tub, pulled her between his spread thighs, held her waist and kissed the bony spot of her sternum. She closed her eyes and swore she'd go to prayer circle with her mother every week as long as no one ever took this moment away.

"Are you okay with this?" he asked, moving side to side, kissing and nipping the plump fleshy curves of her breasts until her thighs trembled with heat.

She nodded, moved her hands to his shoulders for balance. "Oh, yeah. I'm very good with this. *You're* very good with this."

He chuckled, the sound tickling her skin. "Wait till you see what I can do with soap and a sponge."

She was going to die. No way around it. "I'm not sure I'll survive that long."

"I'll stop if you want."

She didn't want. "I'll let you know if I'm in danger of death's door."

"Taking off your socks might help."

"My socks?"

He nodded, his five o'clock shadow scraping her skin, his tongue circling around and around her nipple. "Those are deadly looking."

She smacked the back of his head. He closed his teeth over her in response. A nip, nothing more, but she groaned as the ribbon of pleasure curling through her snapped taut.

"I've had these socks since high school."

"The boxers, too?" he asked, tugging the elastic waistband lower to circle her abdomen at a spot that was dangerously low.

"Yeah. I like feeling comfortable in my things."

"How 'bout feeling comfortable out of your things?" The boxers were barely hanging on her hips by now.

"As long as you don't complain about what you see, I think I can manage a decent comfort level."

He lifted his head from her breasts, dug his thumbs into her pelvis and held her tight. His eyes, when he met her gaze, were heavy with arousal but bright with a spark of what she swore looked like anger.

"Why would you think I would have a goddamn thing to complain about?" he asked, his voice tight as he controlled his response.

"Because I'm definitely less than perfect, and that's what a lot of men seem to want."

"Perfection is in the eye of the beholder, sweetheart. And the best sex is had in the mind. Any man deserving of you would know that."

"Are you that man?"

"I'm working my way in that direction."

"Oh, Tripp," she said with a sobbing sort of

sigh. "How do you manage to make me laugh and cry at the same time?"

"One of my many fine talents."

"Are you going to show me the others now?"

"Only if that's what you want."

She'd never in her life wanted anything more. And so she took a step back, brought down one heel on the toe of the opposite sock and pulled her foot free. The other sock followed in the same fashion, leaving her wearing nothing but the worn boxers. She moved her hands to her waist.

Tripp stopped her with a shake of his head. "I want to do that."

She canted her head to the side and considered him. "Okay, but first I want to see you get out of your clothes."

Twelve

Getting naked had been his plan all along, but when she put it like that . . .

He started with his feet, balancing on one to tug the boot from the opposite, reversing the process until he stood in his socks.

The room smelled like sweet cherries, and he felt like he'd fallen into a strawberry patch, what with the tiled floor of white and red and the matching curtain over the one tiny window.

Then there was Glory, standing with her arms crossed beneath her gorgeous tits, her nipples puckered like raspberries in dark chocolate centers.

He groaned at the sight, his hands going to the hem of his T-shirt, tugging it from his jeans and up over his head. He wadded it into a ball, tossed it on the floor and groaned again for what would probably be only one of a billion times tonight.

She'd shifted her weight from one hip to the other, the stretched waistband of those boxers she wore sliding farther down her body every time she moved, answering his question on their way south.

She wasn't wearing panties at all.

No bikinis, no thong, nothing. He knew that because he could see the barest edge of the strip of dark hair above her sweet pussy lips.

"You're taking too long, Shaughnessey. The water's getting cold."

They were never going to make it into the tub at this rate anyway, so what did it matter?

He unbuttoned the fly of his jeans, shimmied them down his legs. He and Glory now both stood wearing boxers—though his were a lot tighter on his body parts than were hers.

She stepped closer, stopped when she stood at the end of his fingertips' reach, ignored what he'd said about wanting to strip her, and pushed her shorts to the floor.

He was going to come where he stood. His cock bobbed upward, his balls seized up. But it didn't take him two seconds to get as naked as she was.

Or so he thought until she pointed to his socks.

He was out of those puppies in a nanosecond, and then Glory was there, her arms around his neck, her tits flattened against his chest, her thighs open to accommodate his cock that had a heat-seeking mind of its own.

She nuzzled her nose to the side of his. "This feels so nice."

"Yeah," he squeaked out. "Nice."

She pulled back, frowned. "You don't think so?"

"Oh, Glory. If you knew what I was thinking right now . . ."

"Tell me?"

"And ruin a perfectly good fantasy?"

This time, she tilted her head to the side and, smiling, said, "Aren't I your fantasy?"

He slid his hands from where they rested in the small of her back down to cup her ass and squeeze. "All those times I've come into the shop and ordered lunch? I sure as hell wasn't thinking of eating a sandwich."

She blushed, and it was a beautiful sight, the way her cheeks colored like rosy apples. "I knew you were dying for my cake."

"I'm dying now, Glory."

"Then what are you waiting for?"

He backed her into the edge of the tub and pushed her to sit, dropping to his knees between her spread legs. Her thighs shook when he opened her wider. Her hands grew as white as the lip of the porcelain tub onto which she held.

He looked up once, saw that she'd closed her eyes, that she'd caught the edge of her bottom lip between her teeth, and so he lowered his gaze and took in the view he'd been waiting to see.

Her hair was trimmed. That he knew from touching her earlier. What he hadn't known was how dark it was against her soft skin. The lips of her pussy were plumped up, her clit hard and protruding, her juices sparkling there in her slit.

He couldn't wait. His palms on her thighs, he leaned forward and lapped, dipping the tip of his tongue into her hole, dragging the flat part up between her folds. One long, hot hard taste of her and he knew they were both in trouble here.

His cock strained toward his belly, the tip weeping. Glory shuddered until he thought she would tumble back into the tub. Water sloshed over her bottom, between her legs, onto the floor. He wet two fingers with her cream and slid them into her cunt.

She cried out, and he fucked her with his fingers, slowly, steadily, sucked at her clit with the same rhythmic motion, worked her pussy in and out and around, using lips, tongue, the crook and stroke of his fingers until she burst.

It was heat lightning, the sparks arcing between them. She contracted around his fingers, shuddered, trembled, groaned so deeply in her belly his fingers buried deep inside her body vibrated with the sound.

She was exquisite in her pleasure, and he took his time bringing her down, pulling away only when she placed a palm on his head. He got to his feet and she did the same. And then she smiled.

"My turn?" she asked, but he shook his head, scrambled for his jeans and his condoms.

"Sweetheart, as much as I'd love to tickle the back of your throat, there's something I want even more."

"Anything," she said, and he knew she would deny him nothing.

"Bend over."

She got a look in her eye that spoke of a very wicked nature and willingness to please. And then she stood on tiptoe, brushed her lips over his earlobe and whispered, "Take as much as you want."

He closed his eyes and swallowed the urge to shove himself into that mouth. "God, Glory. What are you saying?"

"Exactly what you're hearing, Tripp." And then she turned and presented him with the keys to heaven.

He used one hand to guide his cock to the mouth of her sex and shoved himself forward, waiting for the initial sensation to pass and grabbing hold of her hips for purchase.

She wiggled.

He hissed.

And then he started to move, slowly at first, soaking in her cream and the friction between them. But the temperature grew too hot too fast.

He ground his jaw and picked up the pace, slamming into her like he would take her apart. She moaned, asked for more, begged and pleaded with her mouth as well as with her cunt that gripped his cock so tightly he thought he would die.

It was over before it started. He came in a furious rush of come, unloading into her body until he was spent, drained, and on the edge of falling in love.

"Whew. I'm glad we got that out of the way."

Glory glared at the man sitting across from her in the huge tub and pelted him with her sponge. "Watch the complaints there, Shaughnessey. Or that'll be all you get out of me."

"Say it isn't so," Tripp teased, his expression that of a boy fearing he might never have a chance to snoop around the cookie jar again.

"You play nice, and we'll see how it goes." She leaned into the curve of the tub, drew her heels to her hips and stared at Tripp over the sudsy mountain of her knees. "I can't believe this day. I mean, now it's almost like it was a bad dream, but you're here, so I know it happened."

He arched a surfer blond brow. "You think I wouldn't be here if not for what happened?"

She looked at her knees instead of at him and gave a weak shrug. He tossed the sponge; it hit her square in the chest and she glared. "What was that for?"

"Because you're acting like a woman."

"I am a woman."

"I know that."

Men. Argh! "Then what are you complaining about?"

"A man can only eat so many sprouts in a week, sweetheart. I figured you might realize I was in the shop to see you."

The butterflies were back with a vengeance, and this time she had the advantage of knowing how well he knew how to take care of the tickle. "I just thought you had a thing for turkey and avocado."

He held up a finger. "Don't forget the Dijon."

"And the whole wheat."

"See? You know me as well as I know myself."

"I know what you like to eat." His ego needed no further encouragement, so she twisted her mouth a bit before admitting, "And how well you eat."

He waggled both brows. "Eating is only one of my many talents."

"What are your others?"

He studied her for several long seconds. Apparently she was more transparent than she knew, because he had no trouble seeing her probing intent.

And he wasn't too happy about it. "You're not talking about my sexual prowess, are you?"

"You have prowess?" she teased.

"I have a lot of things that might surprise you."

"I only want to know about one."

"I am a Renaissance man. I do not exist in a single dimension."

"Do you carry a gun?"

That seemed to knock him back a bit. He leaned into the curve of the tub as she had, stretched out his legs until his feet straddled her hips. His knees still broke the water's surface. It was a big tub, but he was a tall man.

"I do, yes. Most of the time."

"Do you have one with you now?"

He shook his head, his mouth in a tight line as if holding in more that he wanted to say.

"What's it like? To use it?"

"I try not to."

"But you have."

He nodded again.

"Well?" She prodded with her toes beneath his thigh as well as with her words.

"It depends on the situation and the outcome, but it's never nice. I mean, I don't go out hoping I'm going to get to use it."

She remembered then that he'd been a sniper. She started to ask, held back, thinking it best to wait before dredging up his past. "Well, I never did think you were an engineer."

"Did I admit that I wasn't?"

She nodded, because what he had said was enough to convince her. "You said you spun webs and leaped tall buildings."

"Have you ever seen a blueprint? If that's not a web . . ."

"An engineer wouldn't think so."

"Hmm. Busted."

"Exactly." She waited, one second, two seconds, hoping he'd say more. When he didn't, she came right out and asked, "What do you do that requires you carry a gun? Are you FBI? CIA? DEA? Some Secret Squirrel government agent?"

"I'm pretty squirrelly, yeah."

Evasive, but cute. "You can't tell me, can you?"

"It wouldn't be a good thing for you to have to admit to your mother."

"My mother?"

"Sure." He scooted forward in the tub, grabbed her by the knees and tugged her between his spread legs. "When you take me home to meet the folks."

"And when am I going to be doing that?" she asked, so close she could see every fleck of color in his eyes.

"I'd say as soon as they start asking questions about the smile on your face."

"My smile?" God, she felt like a mynah bird.

"Yeah. The one your new boyfriend puts there."

She couldn't breathe, her heart was pounding so hard. "I have a new boyfriend?"

"You do now," he said, and covered her mouth with his.

The kiss was long and soft and sweet. He pulled her into the cradle of his body and wrapped her up in his legs. She closed hers behind his hips, felt his penis stir to life against the lips of her sex.

His hands roamed her back with the same testing pressure with which his tongue roamed her mouth. Nothing existed but the here and now for either of them. Nothing but the summer-sweet scent of the room, the warm water lapping like another tongue, the sounds of labored breathing as arousal crept in to blossom and grow.

He was hard between her legs, and she felt herself open with wanting to take him inside. He was in no hurry, however, seeming content to do no more than kiss her, make love to her with his teeth and his tongue, soft thrusts, then bolder, until he released her mouth and went to work along the line of her jaw, her neck, the curve of her ear.

She shuddered and pulled away. "You're making me crazy here, Shaughnessey."

"That's the point, sweetheart." He pulled back, looked into her eyes. "I want you on the verge of crawling out of your skin. And crawling into mine."

Thirteen

"Do you know how long I've wanted you here like this?"

Tripp stared into Glory's eyes, his throat having tightened at her softly spoken question.

They lay naked in her bed, facing each other, playing footsies while their knees touched, both resting up before they tackled cleaning the bathroom.

They'd left one hell of a wet mess on the floor.

"How long?" he finally asked, because it was a safe enough question without first admitting how long he'd wanted to be here.

"Since I'm being honest about my inner slut"—he tickled her low on her belly until she giggled—"I was mentally undressing you the first time you stood there ordering your sprouts."

"Is that so?" This time he tickled her a bit lower, until he felt her moisture seep from between her folds onto the tips of his teasing fingers.

She quivered, nodded in answer to his question, her lower lip caught between her teeth as if she were holding back a whimper or moan she didn't want him to hear.

"And here I thought all that intensity was about trying to get my order right."

"It was. I wanted to make sure you came back."

This time when he tested her wetness, he shifted his hips forward and guided the head of his cock down the seam of her pussy.

This time, he was the one who shuddered.

"Then you did your job well," he said once he'd found his voice. "I couldn't stay away."

"Because of the sandwiches?"

"No, Glory. Because of you."

"Why me?" she whispered as she wrapped exploring fingers around his shaft.

He throbbed into the vise of her hold. "Because you looked at me like you wanted me naked."

"I did not," she denied with a growl, sliding her hand the length of his cock and circling the flat of her palm over the capped head. "I purposefully looked at you like you weren't worth the time of day."

"And aren't you glad I saw right through your ruse?"

"Ha. As if."

"Well, I'm sure not a masochistic glutton for a woman's punishment."

She increased the pressure of her palm, circled the head of his cock repeatedly until he grabbed her by the waist and tumbled her on top of his body. She screeched but settled in and straddled him.

"Stop that," he grumbled. "I'd like to spend some quality time here with you, and it's not going to happen like that."

He raised his knees, and she leaned back, bracing her weight against him, her hands on her thighs, his cock nestled into the soft hair and softer skin between her legs. "Are you going to sleep here tonight?"

It was a simple question. Her tremulous tone of voice and the look in her eyes complicated his answer. He knew what he wanted, but wasn't as certain that she was ready for this to move forward as fast as it seemed to be doing.

Seemed to be, hell. As it had.

"Is that what you want?"

"Is that what you want?"

"Is there an echo in here?"

She growled again—he loved the way the sound vibrated all the way into his body—and she fell forward, catching herself with her hands planted above his shoulders. "Cruisin' for a bruisin' again, Shaughnessey? Because I am definitely in a position here to do some serious harm."

It would take him less than ten seconds to reverse their arrangement, but he loved having her above him, her wild black curls a cloud around her face, her dark cherry nipples both inches from his face.

He moved his hands from beneath his head where he'd tucked his crossed arms, cupped and kneaded her tits until her eyes glazed over and his cock bobbed between their bodies.

"Oh, Tripp, you have no idea how good that feels."

He knew exactly how good his end of the bargain felt. She was sweetly firm and her skin was softer than anything he'd ever rubbed up against. Then there was the tiny fact of how much she wanted him, the way her tongue slipped between her lips when he caught one nipple between two fingers and tugged.

"Yes. I want to spend the night. Whether or not I do is your call," he said before lifting his head and sucking the berry-ripe knot into his mouth.

"Please stay," she begged breathlessly. "In fact, if you never left it would be fine with me."

With his gut clenched and the coals in his belly stirring to life, he swirled his tongue around her, drew her into his mouth, released her to move to the playground of her other breast, but took a second or two to say, "Never's a pretty long time, sweetheart."

When he bit lightly with the barest edge of his teeth and sucked, she cried out, her neck arching as she tossed back her head.

And then she whimpered, "I know. I've never known anyone like you. I've never wanted anyone the way I want you. It's taken way too long for you to get here, Tripp, but I don't want you here if this is all you want from me."

Love at first sight was nothing he'd put much stock in. Hell, he thought, burying his face between her breasts, he wasn't sure love was anything he believed in.

What he did know and what was rapidly becoming apparent, was that he needed to be with this woman as long as she'd have him. And that what he was feeling had dived over the wall separating his comfort zone of lust and the enemy territory of involvement when she'd taken off her clothes in the bathroom.

He made his decision. He dropped his head back to the pillow, looked up into her eyes, and said, "I want to stay. I'll stay as long as you'll have me. And if all we do is cuddle up and sleep, that's fine by me."

She stared down at him, tears giving her eyes a misty sheen. The smile that lifted both corners of her mouth grabbed his heart and squeezed. "Are you just saying that to get me to put out?"

"Hell, yeah," he answered, his vision blurry, a bitch of a frog clogging his throat. "Was it that obvious?"

"It was." She shifted her weight to one arm, slid her free hand down between their bodies, wrapped her tiny cool fingers around his fire-breathing cock. "Especially since you punctuated it with this."

"Oh, well, never let it be said that I'm a master of understatement." And if she didn't let him go, let him breathe, she was going to witness the true power of his punctuation skills.

What she did, instead, was raise up onto her knees and position him exactly where he wanted to be before taking him inside and slowly sliding down into his lap.

He ground his jaw, his eyes rolling back in his head—though averting his gaze didn't do much in the way of helping him find the control she'd crushed with her very light weight.

She leaned forward, placing both palms along his rib cage and massaging her way to his shoulders. The caress was firm, not the least bit hesitant, and would've brought him to his knees if he wasn't already on his back, swaying off balance, on his way to a very big fall.

When she reversed the process, dragging her hands down his torso, her fingertips teasing his nipples as she made her way to his navel where she threaded her fingers into the hair beneath, he couldn't help it. He surged upward, his hips leaving the mattress and taking her with him.

She fell forward, catching herself on his shoulders, one brow arched as she stared down into his eyes. "Punctuating again?"

"In bold and italics."

She chuckled, shook back her hair, then leaned down to kiss him. The spoken conversation had come to an end. Now she was talking with her tongue, teasing it over his lips, dipping it into his mouth.

And she was talking with her hips, rotating and lifting and coming back down until he was a mess of groans and hisses and sounds that had no meaning at all.

He should have been spent by now with all they'd done already, but he felt like he was fifteen, not twice that age, what with the way his cock was throbbing, his balls drawn up into his body, the entire downstairs package ready to blow.

"Glory, sweetheart. It would be really cool here if you'd stop for a second, oh, God, damn, please stop." He poured the words into her open mouth, feeling the heat of his own breath backwash over his face.

Glory stopped moving the part of her body giving him hell, but continued to kiss him, abandoning his lips to tickle his eyelids, eyebrows, his cheekbones, temples and ears, her hands kneading the balls of his shoulders all the while.

And he would've been okay. He would've calmed down and been perfectly fine. The kissing kept him mighty hard, kept him on edge without sending him over.

But as she sat there unmoving, he felt her juices begin to seep out from where their bodies joined and ease down the underside of his shaft.

And that was the end of that.

He hooked an elbow behind her neck, planted a palm in the small of her back, pulled and pressed her down while grinding their mouths and bodies together.

He pumped upward, the friction of sex against sex creating a heat that sent steam to the ceiling. He spread his raised knees, jerked his mouth from hers. She braced her forearms on his chest and curled her fingers into the muscles where his shoulders sloped down from his neck.

It was impossible not to look into her eyes. The room was dark, though she'd left a tiny lamp across the room on her desk burning; the lacy black shawl draped over the shade tossed shadowed shapes onto her skin.

But her eyes were bright with what he swore were tears burning with the same emotion making it impossible for him to speak. All he could do was move, driving, thrusting, pumping and pouring himself into her; sweat broke in the small of her back. He held her there even tighter, his hand slick with desire's perspiration.

She clenched around him then, sucking in a sharp breath as her orgasm hit. He saw that she wasn't ready, that she wanted desperately to wait, to hold on, to make what they were doing last forever.

But he was done. Her contractions were like a fist of fine fingers milking him for all he was worth. And so he gave it up, emptying himself inside her, spilling himself in ribbons of come until he had nothing left to give. Until he felt as if a blade had speared the base of his spine with a pain that was searingly sweet.

He held her tight while she came down, while she learned how to breathe evenly again. While she did her best to dry her tears on a pillowcase, her head turned so he couldn't see.

He didn't have to see. He felt the sobs she tried to suppress, but he didn't say a word. He simply held her, stroked a soothing hand down her back and told her with meaningless noises and whispered nonsense how miserable his life had been without her. How he could lie here beneath her for centuries to come and be the happiest man in the world.

They both must have dozed, because he startled awake when she disengaged their rather sticky bodies a long time later, rolling to his side and draping an arm over his chest.

"Tripp?"

"Glory?"

"Will you answer one question for me?"

"Anything."

"Why do you do what you do?"

The easiest answer of all. "Because if I don't do it, who will?"

Fourteen

Glory finally returned to Brighton's on Monday morning. The police finished their investigation over the weekend and gave her clearance to open for business again. That very business was why she had shown up two hours earlier than she usually did.

She had no idea how much cleanup she'd have to do but knew it would take longer than did her usual morning prep. She was in such a good mood, however, she didn't care how long it took or that she'd be handling most of the lunch rush—what there was of it—on her own.

Knowing it might take customers time to warm up to returning, she'd phoned Neal over the weekend and scheduled his next shift for tomorrow. The time alone didn't faze her at all. In fact, she found herself humming silly love songs and thinking of the last four nights spent with Tripp.

Cliché or not, their time together had been the best of her life. He was fun. And funny. Making her laugh about things she'd never taken the time

to look at before. Like the way she never could fill
an ice tray without spilling. Or how many pairs of
ratty socks she actually had.

Even over the way she liked to spoon backward
when they slept, tucking her knees behind his
thighs and pulling his back to her chest. He said
the whole point of spooning was for her to feel
safe in his arms while she slept. At which point she
reminded him she'd been sleeping alone for a
whole lotta years, and liked the idea of being the
one to offer haven to a man taking on too much of
the world alone.

He'd cuddled back closer, then. Made sure they
were touching everywhere possible. Which eventually led to him taking hold of her hand where it
draped his waist and moving her fingers lower.
The feel of his hard shaft in her palm, the soft, taut
skin of his erection's head beneath her questing
fingers, meant neither of them slept much at all.

Funny thing today was that she wasn't tired at
all. She was too busy to be tired. So busy, in fact,
that it took her a minute to register the opening
and closing of the front door—until the snap of
the blinds being drawn shut doused half the
room's light and brought her head up.

"I'm sorry." She squinted, glanced toward the
door. "I'm not quite . . . open . . . yet . . . oh . . .
God . . ."

Danh Vuong headed her way, wielding a gun
identical to the one he'd wielded on Thursday.

The weapon failed to deter her. She wasn't
going to be a victim again. She snatched up the
phone's handset and ran, punching in 9-1-1. It
wasn't until she put the receiver to her ear that she
realized the line was dead.

She screamed, turned back around, flung the

phone at the approaching man as hard as she could. "What the hell do you want?"

He dodged the phone, but didn't stop or lower the gun. He simply walked straight up to where she stood and shoved the barrel of the weapon against the base of her throat. "It's back into the storeroom for you, Miss Brighton."

She wanted to refuse, to scratch out his eyeballs, to barrel forward and knock him over like a bowling pin. But she was rapidly losing the ability to breathe or to swallow. And so she backed her way down the hallway.

Once he'd shoved her through the door and released her, she rubbed the bruise in the hollow of her throat. "How did you get here? I saw the police take you and your gang out of here."

"You saw them take my associates," he said, one brow raised. "I managed to twist free of my bonds and hide in the same ceiling through which your rescuers arrived."

That didn't make sense. It didn't make sense. "Why didn't they look for you when they only found the five others?"

"Did you tell anyone there were six intruders? Because you were the only one who knew the truth. At least the only one who would've been around to provide the details."

Had she told the police there were six men? Had she mentioned a number?

Or had she been too busy relaying Tripp's story of how Danh's men had turned on one another? How two had disarmed the others. How their leader had taken out those who had betrayed him. How she and the professor had managed to knock him unconscious and bind them all with the zip ties they carried while they were unconscious?

Preposterous, yes. But the professor had backed her up without question. And the physical evidence supported her story. Especially since the police surveillance proved no one had gone in or out through the front, the back, or the side door into the parking garage.

"So now what?" she asked.

"Now I will stand at the front door and turn away all customers but for the one man I am waiting for."

The one from the diamond exchange. "What makes you think he'll show up?"

"Because he's been instructed to. If he does not, I will kill his family."

"You've got to be kidding me." This guy was nuts! "What could you possibly want so badly to ruin so many people's lives?"

"That is not your concern, Miss Brighton."

"But if I'm going to die because of it, I want to know."

He gestured her to back across the storeroom; he stood in the open doorway once she had. "It is about honor, Miss Brighton. About retrieving merchandise stolen from my employer. And about paying my personal debt to him at the same time."

And then he pulled shut the door.

She paced the short room, back and forth, finally slamming her fist into the metal cabinet housing the security screen. The door sprang open, bounced against its own hinges. She watched as Danh passed beneath the camera on his way to the front door.

If only she could signal Tripp's people. But the security service had replaced the cables this morning. She shoved her fingers into her hair and tugged while she whipped around in a circle.

This wasn't happening. This couldn't be happening. Why the hell was this happening? She leaned forward, hands on her knees, to catch her breath.

When she straightened, her gaze landed on the open lip of the Advil box and Tripp's knife lying inside.

"Paperwork is the bane of a man's existence," Tripp grumbled as he filled out an expense report for Smithson Engineering, using bogus travel, entertainment and licensing receipts. He understood the company needed documentation to prove he was earning his keep.

But it was damn hard making up crap for the engineering projects on which he, uh, consulted. It meant traveling to legitimate Smithson sites and bullshitting the project managers so he'd have some clue as to what was going on if asked.

Fortunately, none of the SG-5 operatives were ever asked. Equally fortunate was the fact that none of them truly involved themselves in the construction projects or everything Smithson built would be falling to the ground.

Once Tripp had the backup organized, he printed the expense spreadsheet, attached it, and tossed the envelope across his desk with other mail needing to go out. That left him staring down at the spot where he'd been working at the information he'd dug up on Danh Vuong.

Turned out the kid was a high-ranking officer in the army of one Son Cam, a successful Vietnamese businessman with fingers in a lot of really rotten pies. His street thugs, run by kids like Vuong, handled the messier ingredients, the cleanup of the leftovers, the disposal of the trash.

Danh had been part of Cam's organization for more than half of his twenty-two years; he was younger than Tripp had thought. He'd hitched an illegal ride on a cargo ship, trading in a life of hell for a hell of a life. And right now that life seemed to be all about running Cam's diamond trade.

Tripp rubbed a hand over his forehead, then pressed the heels of both palms to both eyes. He needed to get to this kid, get him off the street, get him for what he did to Glory before he did it to anyone else.

But right now he swore he wasn't going to be getting anything done if he didn't get some sleep. He'd been kept awake for all the right reasons, but the lack of quality shut-eye was still catching up.

With the crap that had gone down at Glory's, he'd lost the Spectra agent posing as Professor Shore. It had gone against every kernel of Tripp's grain to enlist the other man's help. The Faustian bargain meant weeks of surveillance down the drain and a continuing influx of conflict diamonds into Spectra's hands.

But it had also prevented innocent lives from being lost. That, Tripp had to believe.

A hell of a weight, the choices a man made.

He shook off his exhaustion and swung his chair around, pulling up his database on Marian Diamonds. He glanced briefly at the feeds on his surveillance monitors . . .

Holy fucking crap!

He hadn't yet disconnected the Brighton feed—and a damn good thing, too. The picture of Glory's empty shop wasn't the problem; she'd told him she didn't expect her usual business today.

The static was the problem. He'd write that off

to line noise if not for the fact that just then Danh
Vuong walked beneath the camera.

And that the static was pulsing in an SOS.

Where the hell was Glory?

Tripp bounded from his chair, snagged his cell
and his Glock, checked his clip as the safety
vestibule door closed behind him. He sprinted out
of the reception area and down the floor's one
hallway toward the service elevator.

The elevator opened into a maze of tunnel-like
hallways connecting the garage with the Smithson
Building and the one out of which Brighton's op-
erated. He sprinted the length of the corridor,
shoved open the outside door at the end, turned
and ran down the alley toward the sandwich shop's
rear entrance.

He pressed his back against the wall, gun at the
ready, and reached for the door handle. Unlocked.
No resistance. He glanced around, grabbed up a
sheet of newsprint that had blown between his
feet, and wadded it into a ball. Then he eased the
door open and slipped into the shop, wedging the
paper to keep the door from latching completely.

Tamping down the adrenaline pumping through
his body like a rush of meth, he made his way past
the men's room toward the corner and the storeroom door. He listened . . . nothing. No Glory. No
Vuong. He swore he'd stepped into a crypt.

His nostrils flared as one, two, three, he turned,
pressed his torso tight to the wall, peered around
the corner. The vantage point gave him a clear
view all the way to the store's glass front.

Vuong stood to the side of one window, watching the street traffic through a slit in the blinds.

Tripp took one silent step toward the storeroom door, eyes and gun trained on Vuong. The handle turned; he sidestepped into the room, his gaze never leaving Vuong until the door was closed.

He sensed Glory long before he swiveled to meet her gaze. She was gorgeous, amazing, and her eyes were wide with fear. She stood in front of the security cabinet, the newly sliced coaxial cable in her hands.

God, he was crazy for this woman. This time when he mouthed, *I love you*, he meant it. And this time when she mouthed, *I love you, too*, he felt all the pieces of his life fall together.

He held up a halting hand. She nodded, mouthed, *I know. Stay put.*

He took a deep breath, positioned his weapon, slowly pulled open the door—and found himself looking down the barrel of Vuong's gun.

Fuckin' shit on a stick.

Vuong cocked his head to one side, that weird shock of dark hair tumbling onto his forehead. "Mr. Shaughnessey. Why am I not surprised to find you here?"

Tripp sensed Glory moving to stand out of sight beside the shelving unit. "Because you know I'm on your ass like white on rice."

Vuong blinked, frowned, held out his free hand. "Give me your gun."

"I don't think so," Tripp said, mentally scrambling. No one knew where he was. There'd be no backup, no camouflaged cavalry.

Vuong pushed forward into the room, fired off a round above Tripp's shoulder. He flinched, Glory whimpered, but the sound was so soft he was certain Vuong hadn't heard. Was certain the only reason he had was because she was his.

"Give me the gun, Mr. Shaughnessey."

"Not this time, Vuong." A flash of silver glinted in Tripp's peripheral vision.

"Then I'm afraid I have no choice but to kill you."

"You have every choice in the world," Tripp said, sweat running between his shoulder blades. "You're taking the easy way out."

"Easy? You think killing is easy?"

Vuong's response was not what Tripp expected, but was a hot button he would now push because nothing would convince him this man had a conscience. "Sure it is. All you have to do is squeeze the trigger."

Vuong laughed, a dangerously manic sound that echoed like shards of glass falling on the concrete floor. "If you think there is nothing more to killing, then you're not the man I thought you were."

"And if you think there is, then neither are you."

The two men stood face-to-face, guns aimed at one another's chests, chests that rose and fell with their audible breathing. The vein in Vuong's temple looked ready to explode. Time was running out. Tripp felt the spinning second hand in his gut winding down.

All it would take would be one bullet. One twitch of his trigger finger. One decision made in the blink of an eye. He could do it one more time, kill one more man. This was what he'd been trained to do. What he'd done in the jungles of Colombia so many times, he'd lost count.

He saw Glory raise the knife before he could think of the words to stop her. She lunged, hands clasped overhead, swinging down in an arc, bury-

ing the blade to the hilt in the slope of Vuong's
shoulder.

His eyes shot wide, he twisted. Tripp brought
his wrist down on Vuong's gun hand, his knee up
on the elbow.

Crack!

Vuong went down in writhing silence. The gun
spun across the room, hit the far wall, and went
off. Glory screamed and ducked. Tripp jumped
back, his pulse exploding, staring down at the gaping chasm where the kid's neck had been. *Jesus!*
Blood pooled on the floor, Vuong's expression an
agonizing death mask that softened into an eerie
childlike face.

Tripp stepped over the downed man and did
the only thing that mattered right now. He took
Glory in his arms and squeezed until even he was-
n't able to breathe, guiding her from the room,
pulling the door closed behind him.

He didn't stop until they were standing em-
braced in the center of the shop. He'd call the cops
in a minute. Or two. Or three. When he could think
to explain what had happened. When he could
think beyond the fact that Glory was safe.

"Amazing, amazing, amazing." It was all he
could say, his voice hoarse and ragged, his throat
closing around a ball of emotion the likes of which
he swore he would never survive.

"Did you mean it this time?" she whispered into
his shirt, tears wetting him, her heartbeat synced
with his. "About loving me?"

"Oh, goddamn yes, I meant it. I am out of my
mind over you." There. He'd said it. And he'd gotten it out around that damn frog squatting in his
throat.

"Oh, Tripp." Her arms tightened further where

she'd wrapped up his waist. "I couldn't stay put. I just couldn't."

"Shh, sweetheart. You did good. You did just fine."

She sniffed. "For a girl without super powers, you mean?"

"Oh, Glory." He tucked her head beneath his chin, cupped the back of her head and held her. He couldn't manage another word. He could barely breathe. He stared at the clock on the wall, at the second hand ticking its way the length of the pickle and back.

"You don't need super powers. You have me." Then he closed his eyes and mind to everything but Glory. "And I have you."

The

SAMMS

AGENDA

A man can stand a lot as long as he can stand himself. He can live without hope, without friends, without books, even without music, as long as he can listen to his own thoughts.

—Axel Munthe, 1857–1949
Swedish physician,
psychiatrist, and writer

One

Turning heads was something Katrina Flurry had done constantly throughout the twenty-eight years of her life. She wasn't going to apologize for it, defend it, or get bent out of shape when it didn't sit well with what girlfriends she had left.

She'd never been one to play up her looks, but she'd certainly never had a reason to play them down. Especially now that they were one of the only things left she had going for her. Sad that such was the state of things, but running from the truth went against her personal grain.

Even if lately she'd given the idea of running a whole lot of thought.

Her looks had played a big part in her successful entrée into the social circles about which she wrote. In fact, her syndicated urban lifestyle column, *Cosmopolitan Arm Candy,* ran in a multitude of publications along with a caricature that looked enough like her to stop traffic dead.

And speaking of dead . . .

She swung her legs over the side of her lounger, slipped her feet into her poolside slides, and packed her towel, sunscreen, and the paperback she'd been reading into her tote, wondering as she gathered up her things if her ex, the worthless bastard, had yet been sent to meet his maker.

It was true that Peter Deacon had provided amazing fodder for her column. And she wasn't about to deny how much she'd enjoyed spinning through the circles of society in which he'd traveled.

What she hadn't enjoyed was discovering two months ago that the man she'd dated for the six months prior wasn't who she'd thought he was at all.

That he was, in fact, the front man for the sort of crime syndicate that brought to mind James Bond movies and Elmore Leonard books—and which made her, ugh, his moll.

A mobster's girlfriend. What a lovely experience to add to her resumé.

She wondered with a rather grim satisfaction how Peter was enjoying his traveling now, from his cell to the prison mess hall and on to the caged exercise yard.

The thought of his well-manicured hands working to press license plates . . .

She leaned down to check the scuffed polish on one toe, feeling the zip of a bee zinging by her ear as she bent. Dodging the insect and cupping that side of her head, she swore never again to spend a free afternoon poolside after a morning pedicure.

Now she was going to need a touch-up before tonight's charity fund-raiser hosted by the Miami Symphony. She was so looking forward to an evening spent at the fabulous Mandarin Oriental without the odious and criminal Peter Deacon at her side.

Okay, she mused wryly, getting to her feet. She hadn't found him odious while they were seeing each other. At the time, however, she'd had no idea of his true colors—colors that were now limited to black and white horizontal stripes, or whatever dazzling combination was worn by the population at Sing Sing.

Considering she would never be paying him a visit, she contented her imagination with picturing him thus—when she pictured him at all, an event growing more and more rare of late.

Adjusting the rise of her bikini bottoms, she reached for her cover-up and slipped it on, tightening the kimono's sash around her waist.

As much as she wished she could wipe him from her mind completely, a part of her harbored no small degree of guilt . . . or anger . . . or disgust—she had yet to define the emotion—that he'd pulled the wool over her eyes until she saw nothing but soft and cuddly sheep.

It was tough accepting that she'd been such a bad judge of character when she prided herself on the opposite.

She reached down for her tote, cringing again as that damn bee buzzed the hairs on the back of her neck. A big red welt of a sting would ruin the effect of the plunging ivory and gold silk halter topping the slim ankle-length Cleopatra skirt it had taken her hours to choose for tonight.

The fund-raising event was dreadfully important to her personal future as it was the first society function she would be attending unescorted since Peter's arrest.

The gossip would be flowing as freely as the Veuve Clicquot and Pol Roger, and squashing rumors of her knowledge of his true business dealings was her main goal for the evening.

She had not been a party, knowing, willing, or otherwise, to his unscrupulous activities, and she had certainly known nothing about his treasonable crimes.

Even now she shuddered and swallowed the bile that rose when she thought of the young scientist who'd burned to death in that fire in upstate New York. Rumor had the kid as deeply involved as Peter had been, but no one deserved such a horrific end.

At the moment, though, it was her own reputation on the line, her own future suffering the collateral damage of Peter's reach.

Courtney David, Katrina's editor at her home base of the *Miami Herald,* had warned her earlier in the week to expect a possible backlash. Two of the more conservative markets running *Cosmopolitan Arm Candy* had already put her column on hiatus until the hoopla of her involvement with Peter died down.

Repositioning her sunglasses, Katrina admitted she had a hell of a fight ahead. What her doubters and detractors didn't know was that fighting—and winning—was the hallmark of all Flurry women.

She would not lose the career she'd worked her ass off to establish without a serious battle royal and a lot of metaphorical dead bodies left in her wake.

It was when the bee buzzed her again and smashed into one of the poolside's Grecian urn planters that she realized the first dead body might very well be hers. Because that bee was no bee.

It was a bullet.

* * *

"Tzao gao," swore Julian Samms under his breath, the fluid burst of Mandarin as natural as picking the lock on the front door of Katrina Flurry's condo.

He wasn't worried about being caught on tape by the high-tech security system. Even a zoom shot would show him opening the door with what looked like a key.

Besides, though she didn't yet know it, Katrina Flurry didn't live here anymore.

And if he didn't get her out of Miami now, she wouldn't be living at all.

Spectra IT, the international crime syndicate tailor-made to employ scum like Peter Deacon, had put out a hit on the man's former girlfriend, using the assassin most suited to a job involving a sexy woman and a gun: Benny Rivers.

Julian knew way too much about Benny's penchant for abhorrent sexual torture. The other man was an equal opportunity sadist, meaning no man, woman, or sheep was safe from the abuse and humiliation he doled out before death.

Hank Smithson, the founder and principal of the Smithson Group, had sent Julian to make sure Katrina avoided that scenario while Mick Savin, Hank's newest SG-5 recruit, put his bloodhound nose to Benny's foul trail.

If the game went according to plan, and she didn't put up an uncooperative stink in the process, Julian would have Katrina tucked safely away thirty minutes from now.

He knew from his surveillance that she was home; he'd hoped a simple knock would've been enough to gain him entrance. But no. Either she wasn't opening up because she hadn't recognized him, or because she was busy in her closet alphabetizing her shoes by designer.

He had absolutely no problem with quality footwear; he had a problem with any obsession resulting in waste of any kind—physical, mental, emotional, or spiritual.

The fact that she could afford a real-life *Sex and the City* wardrobe had no impact on his opinion. But then, nothing ever did. Nothing ever would.

Not after what he'd witnessed during the two years he'd spent stationed in Africa.

And on that last deadly assignment in Kenya.

He'd read several installments of her syndicated column during his mission prep. *Cosmopolitan Arm Candy.* What a load of high-maintenance *gou shi*. The fact that she had the readership she did left him speechlessly shaking his head at the state of female affairs.

If women thought men gave a rat's ass about external trappings, they were out of their airheaded minds.

Men who were real men cared about two things. A woman able to carry on an intelligent conversation filled with innuendo and mind games, who then delivered an equally fulfilling challenge once she joined him in bed.

The makeup and jewelry and shoes and nails? Uh-uh. His experience told him those were tools used to impress other women and for gaining an edge in the self-esteem war games females played.

Why they felt the strangely competitive need to best one another with the superficial trappings of class . . . He gave another shake of his head as the door came open in his hand.

He didn't want to walk in and find himself facing the wrong end of the handgun registered in her name, so he knocked again as he cracked open the door. "Miss Flurry?"

He peered into the foyer. *Whoa. Nice digs,* he mused, stepping onto white-and-black marbled Italian tile. He knew from his background research that Katrina came from money, that her father had died while she was in high school, leaving wife and daughter financially set for the rest of their lives.

His bitching about her wardrobe budget aside, he had to admire her taste. Talk about quality. He'd even give her elegance. Her place deserved a spread in *Architectural Digest.* He figured her square footage at two thousand at least—not a bad bit of acreage for one person to move around in.

She went for what he supposed was classical, or traditional, the sort of décor that didn't exactly invite anyone to sit, to ditch their shoes, to kick back with a beer and spend Sunday afternoon watching football—a nonissue since the room didn't have a television and he wouldn't fit on her red and gold brocade camelback sofa anyway.

You're a moron, Samms. You're not a fixture in her condo or in her life. And it would never be so with any woman, a fact his subconscious was still warring over with his logic all these years later.

A cursory walk-through of her kitchen yielded no Katrina, no dirty dishes, and nothing on the stove. A perverse part of him wanted to check her refrigerator, see if it was stocked with fruits, vegetables, yogurt, and designer-label water, but the unsealed package of Chunky Chips Ahoy on the countertop changed his mind. Not to mention intrigued him.

He liked the idea of this gourmet woman having a few pedestrian tastes. It made him wonder how she'd feel about eating those cookies in bed—

yet another mental detour he had no business taking.

He made his way over the plush ivory carpet toward the private rooms of the condo. "Miss Flurry?"

Still nothing, and yeah, he'd been right on the mark with his earlier assessment of the money she spent on shoes. Standing at the door to her monstrous closet, he estimated she owned a hundred pair.

A regular mini-Imelda.

And he really shouldn't be checking out her wardrobe, but it was either that or the bed. The bed which made him think about those cookies and how he could really go for a night of down and dirty sex.

He headed back to the living room and the balcony that opened over the courtyard pool. The fitness center and tennis courts would be his next destination since he knew she employed a housekeeper and wouldn't be doing her own laundry in the center's facilities . . .

There she was, down at the pool, her back to him as she got to her feet and tugged at a pair of bikini bottoms that sent his libido back to the idea of leaving cookie crumbs in her bed.

She'd coiled her shoulder-length caramel-colored hair into a knot on top of her head. He liked the length of her neck almost as much as he liked the length of her legs.

What he wasn't crazy over was the way she was covering up without first turning around so he could get a full frontal view of that body. Then again, her body was merely a perk of this job, not the reason he was here.

She looked like she was on her way back upstairs, meaning he'd do better to intercept her on the other side of her front door. Save himself a buttload of explaining—who he was, how he'd gotten in, what he wanted, as well as the hassle of having to restrain her when she refused to listen.

Cookies or not, she struck him as the type to act first and ask questions a mile or so down the damn road.

In the next second, however, the insect she'd been dodging shot his carefully laid plans to shit when the cement planter it hit exploded. Julian whipped his gaze to the rooftop across from where he stood.

Sunlight cast Benny Rivers's block-like head in silhouette, and glinted off the barrel of the rifle aimed her way.

Katrina's only saving grace for the moment was that Rivers never gave his prey an easy time, toying with his victims, making them sweat out the wait for their death.

Heart pounding in the base of his throat, Julian gauged the distance from the balcony to the manicured lawn edging the poolside walk, gauged the distance to the deep end of the crystal blue water shimmering in the sun, chose the lesser of two evils, and jumped.

Two

Julian hit the ground with a jolt, seams ripping, bones crunching, joints popping as he rolled to his feet and came up into a full-throttle run.

Coattails flying, he sprinted across the pool's cement deck, hurdled the shattered planter, and gave Katrina no chance to do more than gasp her surprise as he grabbed her upper arm and ran.

"Go! Go! Go! Go! Go!"

He propelled her forward, knowing he could run a hell of a lot faster then she could, the both of them dragged down even more by the *slap, slap, slap* of her ridiculous shoes.

She seemed to reach the very same conclusion at the very same time, however, and kicked off the slides to run in bare feet.

Once across the deck and up the courtyard stairs, he shoved open the enclosure's gate. Another bullet ricocheted off the iron railing.

Katrina screamed, but kept up with the pace he

set as they pushed through and barreled down the arched walkway toward the parking garage.

Her Lexus was closer, but he doubted she had her keys and didn't have time to stop, ask, and wait for her to dig them from the bottom of her bag.

Even breaking in, hot-wiring would take longer than the additional burst of speed and extra twenty-five yards they'd need to reach his Benz.

"My car. Let's go," he ordered.

She followed, yelping once, cursing once, twice, yet sticking by his side all the way.

A shot cracked the pavement to the right of their path, a clean shot straight between two of the garage's support beams. Way too close for comfort.

Rivers's practice was about to make perfect in ways Julian didn't want to consider.

The keyless transponder in his pocket activated the entry into his car from three feet away. He touched the handle, jerked open the SL500's driver's side door.

Katrina scrambled across the console, tossed her bag onto the floor; he slid down into his seat, punched the ignition button, shoved the transmission into reverse.

Tires screaming, he whipped backwards out of the parking space and shot down the long row of cars. He hit the street ass-backwards, braked, spun, shifted into first, and floored it, high-octane adrenaline fueling his flight.

Halfway down Grand, several near misses and an equal number of traffic violations later, he cast a quick sideways glance at Katrina and nodded. "You might want to buckle up."

She cackled like she'd never heard anything more ridiculous. "You're suggesting that now?"

He shrugged, keeping an eye on his rearview

and any unwanted company, whether Rivers or the cops. He wasn't about to stop for either. "Better late than never."

That earned him a snort, but she did as she'd been told. Then she lifted her left foot into her lap, giving him an eyeful of a whole lotta tanned and toned thigh. "I've got glass in my foot."

He didn't say anything. He had to get out of her neighborhood and ditch his car—a reality that seriously grated. "Stitches?"

She shook her head, leaning down for a closer look at the damage. "I don't think so. Tweezers, antibiotic ointment, and a bandage should suffice."

"I've got a first aid kit in the trunk." How many times had he patched himself up on the fly? "I'll grab it as soon as we stop. In the meantime . . ." He pulled his handkerchief from his pocket.

"Thanks." She halved it into a triangle and wrapped her foot securely, knotting the fabric on top at the base of her toes. "When you hit 95, head south. The police station's on Sunset."

He nodded, and turned north at the next intersection.

"Uh, hello? I said Sunset. South, not north."

"I heard you." This wasn't the time for a long explanation as to why he couldn't go to the police, why SG-5 couldn't risk exposure.

Why he'd learned a long time ago that actions spoke a hell of a lot louder than words.

"Look," she said, settling her sunglasses that he happened to know were Kate Spade firmly in place. "I appreciate the save, even if I was dumb as a stick to get in this car not knowing who you are. But we're going to the police, or I'll be making a scene like you wouldn't believe."

Oh, he believed Miss High Maintenance capable of something that *feng le* . . . crazy. So far the only surprise had been her lack of complaints over their full out hundred-yard dash and the injury she'd sustained in the process.

"This isn't a police matter." Still, heading in the direction of the station might keep Rivers at bay and give Julian time to consider his options.

"And why would that be?" she asked, her incredulous tone of voice unable to mask the sound of the gears whirring in her mind. "You're with the shooter, aren't you? This kidnapping was the goal all along. You sonofabitch."

Julian couldn't help it. He smiled. It was something he rarely did for good reason, and the twitch of unused facial muscles felt strange.

But there was just something about a woman with a sailor's mouth that grabbed hold of his gut and twisted him up with the possibilities.

He hadn't had a really good mouth in a very long time.

A thought that sobered him right up. "No. I'm not with the shooter. His name is Benny Rivers. He's with Spectra IT and he's in Miami to take you out."

Take her out. As in . . . kill her?
Dead?

"Who are you?" she asked, her pulse fluttering like it hadn't since she'd first learned the truth of Peter Deacon's affiliations.

Fluttering harder, in fact, if fluttering was even the right word considering if felt like a jackhammer pounding away in her chest. "What do you want?"

"What I want is to keep you alive." He shifted

down, revved his RPMs. The car shot up the ramp onto I-95. "Who I am isn't as important."

"Uh, if my life is in danger then what's important is my call to make." Her foot began to throb, the glass shard suddenly taking on the dimensions of a Fifth Avenue window in Bergdorf's.

"My name is Julian Samms," he finally answered in that voice that sounded like honey poured over a shattered mirror. Smooth and ragged all at the same time.

"Julian Samms. And you're simply an ordinary average concerned citizen?" He was obviously nothing of the sort.

Was, in fact, much much more, what with his very sophisticated James Bond attire, not to mention his car, which was worth a small fortune, and his skill behind the wheel.

Ordinary average concerned citizens did not drive like highly trained bats out of hell.

"Something like that," he responded, whipping through traffic with one eye trained on his mirrors, one hand on the wheel, and the other on the gear shift as he searched the road behind.

She wanted to glance back, to see what he was looking for, but what really mattered was what lay ahead. "Where are we going?"

"I'm not sure."

"What do you mean, you're not sure?" How could he have been in the right place at the right time and not be sure of what he was doing now?

"Exactly what I said." Another in-and-out maneuver that had her grabbing hold of the door. "All I know is that I've got to get you out of Miami."

"For how long?"

"As long as it takes."

"As long as what takes?"

The glance he cast her way accused her of asking too many stupid questions for a woman on the run for her life.

Logically, she knew that. Emotionally . . .

"I can't leave. I work here. I live here," she said, hysteria adding an ugly shrillness to her voice. And tonight was the fund-raiser!

He ignored her panic and simply said, "You used to live here."

No. She was not going to listen to this or go down without a fight.

She was already struggling to regain the personal and career footing she'd lost by having her name linked with an international crime figure.

And at that thought . . .

Dear God, but she was in serious trouble here, wasn't she? More trouble than she'd been willing to accept until it was slapped brutally across her face like a bullwhip.

Or like a bullet.

She slumped back, deflated, defeated, yet determined to find a better solution than one calling for her to give up everything she still held dear.

"I don't understand why we can't go to the police." She didn't understand anything at all! "Surely they could provide me protection."

Julian snorted. "The same way they provided you protection from Rivers?"

"How could they when they didn't know . . . ?"

But he had known. Julian Samms had known. Which brought her back to the moment's biggest conundrum.

Who the hell was this dangerous man and what about him made her feel safe when the circumstances should have her feeling anything but?

She shifted in her seat as best she could to face

him, studying his profile as he concentrated on the traffic and the road.

The shoulder seam of his black Hugo Boss suit was torn, the fabric separating now as his muscles bunched while he shifted gears, revealing the white shirt he wore, also torn and showing a hint of deeply tanned skin underneath.

She couldn't tell much about his body beyond the fact that he ran a hell of a lot faster than she would've imagined for a man of his size. He was very large. Intimidatingly so.

Or would have been had she been put off by physical strength.

She never had been, she mused, the faint hum of the wheels on the pavement belying the speed at which they traveled. Since childhood, she'd used her wits to get out of any scrapes she'd been in, believing brains won out over brawn every time.

She believed it still to this day. And she needed to employ the same wits now she had then, but wasn't having as easy a time of it.

As far as she knew, no one had ever tried to kill her before.

"Do you have any sort of plan then?" she finally asked, because staring at the thick dark hair pulled into a tail at his nape was getting her nowhere.

His answer was a sharp vocal burst in a language she did not understand and an equally sharp spin of the steering wheel. The movement took them across all the lanes of traffic, down the exit ramp, and into the parking lot surrounding the Shops at Sunset Place.

He slipped the car into a spot between two oversized SUVs, set the emergency brake, and left the car idling in neutral. "We've got to switch cars."

She could help with that, she realized. She

could finally help with something. "I can get us a car."

His head swiveled her way. His blue eyes burned beneath brows even blacker than his hair. But it was the tight line of his lips, the stress brackets on either side of his mouth that drew her gaze.

"What sort of car and where?"

She shook her head. She obviously wasn't going to draw this out, but there were things she needed to know.

And she needed to know them now. "I'll tell you. As soon as you answer a few questions for me."

Three

Julian never talked about who he was, where he'd come from, what he did. "What sort of questions?"

"I would think that would be obvious," she said, the defensive arch of her brow a tactical maneuver made to unbalance him.

It failed, of course, ramping up his curiosity about her instead.

He wondered if she thought the look was enough to mask the swell of fear she was riding. He knew fear, recognized it, would've smelled it on her if not for all the other scents swirling in the car's interior.

Sunscreen and sweet soap and the soft citrus tang of her hair.

When it became clear that he wasn't going to answer what he hadn't been asked, both her expression and her tone of voice shifted from imperious to insistent.

"Who are you that you know more about Spectra IT's activities than the police do?"

"The group I work for . . ." He hesitated, not wanting to say enough to give away SG-5 but knowing she deserved this much of the truth—needed it, in fact, if they were both to stay alive. "One of my associates is responsible for taking your ex out of commission."

She blinked once, twice, her lashes long, sable dusted with gold. "Are you government? Military?"

He shook his head. "Not any longer."

"I don't get it," she said, her eyes reflecting the anger and confusion warring behind them. "I mean, I understand what you're doing here, but I don't get who sent you or why or who you work for—"

"You don't need to get it. All you need to do is stay alive until Rivers is disposed of." That and follow his orders without the back talk and sass he'd geared up for. Neither of which he'd yet seen.

She met his gaze squarely, her chin quivering so slightly he doubted she noticed. "And that's where you come in, right? The keeping me alive part."

He nodded. It was Mick Savin who would be disposing of Benny Rivers, though Julian still wasn't clear why Hank had given the new recruit the meatier task while assigning him to baby-sit.

He draped his left wrist over the steering wheel and tried not to notice the way the diamond studs in her ears glittered, or the way her topknot sat askew, strands of hair curling wildly the length of her neck.

Caramel strands. Caramel and chocolate. Chocolate chip cookies. He stifled a groan. "Anything else?"

She canted her head, looked down and picked at the handkerchief bandage. "We only dated casually. Peter and I. We were never a romantic item."

"Right." Julian turned his head, moved his gaze

to the rearview mirror, searching for any possible sign of Rivers instead of divining the truth from her eyes.

That particular truth, her relationship with Deacon, didn't matter.

"I never slept with him."

Her soft confession had Julian grinding his jaw. "Sure. Whatever."

She sighed with a heavy sense of even heavier frustration. "I hate people thinking that more went on between us than actually did."

It didn't matter, he told himself again. *It didn't matter.* Her association with and her obvious attraction to the Spectra sleazebag was enough to turn Julian right off, chocolate chip cookies aside.

He drummed his fingertips on the dash. "What about the car?"

"My mother lives in Coral Gables. She's in London visiting friends. I have keys to her place and to her car."

"You have them with you?"

She muttered a faint string of foul words under her breath. "No. They're at my condo."

"Rivers will be watching the place anyway."

"How would he know—" She cut herself off before saying more, took a deep breath. "Never mind. I'm just glad she's not there."

If she had been, Julian would've taken measures to keep her out of harm's way. "Don't worry about it. The car part, I mean."

Again she pulled at the knot on the bandage. "I thought you covert types always had contingency plans."

His plan had been to set her up in a safe house until Rivers was no longer an issue. A safe house hidden on the tip of the peninsula that put SG-5 within spitting distance of Spectra's offshore activities.

The plan remained the same. It was Rivers who was going to make the execution tougher than Julian had hoped.

He pulled his cell phone from his waistband and hit his speed dial.

"Savin."

"It's Julian. Rivers is here. I just lost him on 95 out of Coconut Grove."

"Great." Mick bit off a sharp laugh. "Because I lost him up at Okeechobee."

"You'll be here soon?"

"Less than an hour."

"Good. *Zhu yi.*"

"Yeah. You watch your back, too."

Julian slapped the phone closed. "Sit tight. I'm going to get the first aid kit."

She nodded, her eyes as dry as the Chalbi Desert he knew too well. He pushed from the car, opened the trunk, thinking of the dry barren waste and the sun cooking a man's skin to a fiery red crisp.

Not toasting it to a golden brown tan that went on forever, inside her thighs and out, all the way to the scrap of parakeet yellow fabric between her legs that he knew would be sheer when wet.

It was the thinking of making her wet that had driven him from the car even more than the glass in her foot.

She wasn't his type—he'd met few women who were—but he was a man, and she was wearing next to nothing and smelling like sunshine and—*zing!*

Hun dan!

Sonofabitch! The bullet pierced the wheel well, whacked into the passenger door of the neighboring SUV.

Julian slammed the trunk, curses rolling from his tongue as he dashed forward. He threw the first aid kit into Katrina's lap, shifted into reverse, and whipped back out of the parking space.

He shot blindly down the row of parked cars, skidding into a ninety-degree turn at the end of the row. They'd be nothing but a moving target on 95, but getting to the safe house was paramount.

Pulse pounding, he tore out of the lot on what felt like two wheels, hit the lane to the interstate's entrance ramp prepared to top out the roadster at its 360 kilometers per hour.

Katrina dug fingertips into his thigh and stopped him with a manic, "U-turn! U-turn! Go back!"

He did what she said. She couldn't believe he'd done what she said—even as she swore she'd saved both their lives. God, but she could barely think to breathe.

She'd seen the hell-bent-for-leather expression darkening his face and feared he'd flip this rocket of a car, killing them both.

With that scenario now on hold, she directed him off the S. Dixie at the 8th Avenue exit and had him turn east.

"Little Havana?"

"My mother and I employ the same housekeeper. We can use her car." She hesitated. "And leave her yours."

The glance he cast her remained indecipherable even after he'd returned his gaze to the road.

But the intensity stuck with her, and she couldn't help but wonder what he was thinking, considering he knew only the more salacious parts of her past.

"Besides, I've got to get clothes." On this she would not budge.

Nothing about the way he'd looked at her had been the least bit improper. But she could hear him breathe and sensed a tight discomfort, as if the distance between them was too little.

Or maybe too much.

She directed him through the neighborhood; his car, as she'd known it would do, turned heads, drawing more attention than she could tell he liked. The quick twists and turns they took through the narrow streets, however, would make their vanishing act hard to follow.

"Turn in here." She indicated Maribel's driveway. The housekeeper's sedan was parked at the curb. The one-car garage was empty. "Pull into the garage."

She answered the question asked by his dark expression. "Maribel's husband Tomas parks his truck in here. But I promise he won't mind if we store your car for now."

He eased the Mercedes roadster into the tiny pocket of space between tarps, ladders, plastic sheeting, and cans of paint.

He cut off the engine with the touch of a button, leaving her listening to the sound of her own heartbeat and what she swore was the equally rapid thrumming of his.

She wanted to turn to him, to demand more details than the scant ones he'd provided, to lean into the curve of his shoulder and rest her head. To pull the leather band from his nape and watch his thick black hair fall to frame his high cheekbones and strong jaw and . . .

Oh-kay. Enough with the fantasy. Time to get out of the car and start getting her life back, though she supposed tonight's fund-raiser was now out of the question. Damn but she'd looked good in that Cleopatra dress.

And damn that her nonappearance tonight would set additional tongues to wagging, creating more controversy she'd have to deal with eventually.

Feeling sorry for herself, however, was hardly productive when bigger things than her dress and reputation were being threatened. She wasn't exactly thrilled to add experience with gunfire and high-speed chases to her resumé.

Not to mention dealing with this ridiculous attraction to a man she wasn't yet sure was captor or savior.

The pit of her stomach tingling, she hobbled from the car to the backyard's chain-link gate. Holding the first aid kit in one hand, her tote in the other, she worked up the gate's horseshoe closure.

Behind her, Julian pulled down the garage's one-piece door. By the time she'd reached Maribel's back porch and knocked, he'd joined her. When nobody answered, she knocked again.

"She's usually home on Fridays. Should we wait?"

"No." He reached into his suit coat's inside pocket, withdrew a thin leather pouch stocked with what looked like dentistry tools but she knew were lock picks. "We're going in."

Four

Katrina followed him through the door with no small amount of trepidation. Maribel would not mind in the least having them inside her house.

But the idea of breaking and entering like a common criminal did not sit well.

The white clapboard home's back entrance led directly into a small kitchen that was spotless. Knowing Maribel, Katrina expected no less.

She'd only been here once before, having brought food to the Gonzalez family when the housekeeper was called away by a relative's sudden death.

The gold-flecked linoleum was worn but waxed; the icebox and range both white enamel and from another era, functioning long past their prime.

The sink was white enamel, as well, chipped in spots but without a single stain. Katrina could see it all from where she still stood just inside the doorway.

Apparently much less ill at ease making his un-invited self at home, Julian vanished into the depths of the small house. Katrina limped her way to the kitchen's Formica dinette set, pulled out a chair, and sat.

Placing her tote and the first aid kit on the table-top, she lifted her foot to her lap and slipped off the knotted and bloody handkerchief.

Her foot was throbbing to beat the band. A quick inspection showed the sliver of glass to be a lot bigger and more deeply embedded than she'd thought.

Not that any thought beyond staying alive had been involved when she'd first felt the glass pierce her skin.

Sighing, she unzipped the canvas kit and had just found the tweezers when Julian tossed his torn shirt and coat across the table.

She glanced from the garments in need of re-pair to his face—but didn't make it that far. The heavy white T-shirt he'd pulled on to wear with his suit pants was all she could see.

No. That wasn't quite true. What filled her vi-sion was the amazing expanse of his chest and the width of his shoulders poured into a shirt far too small.

He sat in the chair at a right angle to hers. Po-liteness forced her gaze to his face.

It was the clearest look she'd had of him so far, and she swore without hesitation that she'd never have climbed into his car if she'd seen him like this.

He'd pulled the band from his hair and the strands now hung to his shoulders; the color wasn't the pure black she'd thought, but a shade of brown just this side of it.

He patted his thigh. "Let me see your foot."

She lifted her heel to his knee, all too aware that she was wearing next to nothing and tucking the edges of the kimono as best she could over her thighs. "It's worse than I thought. I still don't think it needs stitches, but I'm not looking forward to digging for the glass."

Julian wrapped his fingers around her toes, bent them back gently and tilted her foot. He studied the injury for a moment then turned to search the kitchen counters.

Katrina watched his face, ignoring the pressure and warmth of his fingers that had slipped down to ring her ankle. At least she told herself she was ignoring his touch.

Not that she believed anything she said considering the gooseflesh pebbling the entire length of her leg.

"Hang on a sec." He lifted her foot to the tabletop and pushed to stand, heading for the paper towels hanging from a roller next to the stove and the bottle of Cuervo Gold on top of the fridge. He didn't bother with glasses or ice.

It was when he sat down again that she realized the tequila was for her foot.

He braced the roll of paper towels on his thigh, reached for her heel, and propped it on top, scooting closer until her toes, if she flexed them, could tickle his ribs.

Flexing wasn't in the cards. Not when any movement now spit fire over the ball of her foot. She sucked in a sharp breath as Julian opened the bottle.

"This is gonna burn like a mother."

She gripped the aluminum edging along the seat of her chair and grit her teeth. "Bring it on."

He held her foot in one hand, held the bottle

suspended in his other, and hesitated a moment while he also held her gaze.

His lips twitched with what might've been a spot of admiration. Unless it was devilish mischief. "Don't say I didn't warn you."

She stared into his eyes, the blue of a midnight sky. Blue and twinkling like those of a kid holding a match in one hand, a Black Cat in the other, and wondering if he could outrun the blast.

Interesting considering her insides seemed to be burning a similar fuse. A life-affirming sizzle detonating in the face of death. Oh, but this day was so not going well.

She inhaled deeply. "Hit me, bartender."

He poured. The alcohol ran from the ball of her foot down her sole and over her ankle to soak into the thick roll of towels. She wanted to scream but she couldn't. Not with Julian still holding her gaze.

Instead, she lifted one brow, gripped the chair even tighter, and nodded her permission for him to dig in. He took up the tweezers . . . and she never felt a thing.

He was good. Damn good. "I'm guessing you've had medic experience? More than simple Red Cross first aid?"

"I've seen a few guys get patched up, yeah. By medics, and by the Red Cross. None of it simple."

His attention on her foot, he wouldn't have noticed her silent touché. She offered it nonetheless. "How long were you in the service?"

He gave a strange shrug of his shoulders. "Six years. Almost."

She hissed sharply as the tweezers' tips grated over the edge of the glass. "That would be it."

"So it seems." He frowned, his dark brows drawing her attention to his eyes, to his nose, down to his lips.

He'd pressed them together as he concentrated; all she could think about was how much she wanted to kiss them. "Why almost?"

"Hmm?" He pulled the glass free, pressed his thumb to the gash to staunch the bleeding. "Why almost what?"

The pressure he applied created only marginally less pain than the glass. But it was a pain offset by the ridiculous pleasure his hands offered.

Good grief. What was the matter with her? "Why almost six years in the service?"

"You're going to need to be stitched up, but this will have to do for now." He replaced his thumb with a gauze pad. "Hold this a sec."

She leaned forward, held the gauze, watched while he uncapped the antibiotic ointment. His movements were precise and efficient as was his side of the conversation, an economy of words used to tell her nothing.

All he had to do was tell her to shut the hell up and quit asking questions, the answers to which were none of her business.

Then again, she mused, wincing only once as he applied the dressing, she was obviously projecting what she would be thinking were their positions reversed.

So it came as no small surprise when, while packing the items back into the kit, he said, "I was discharged. Dishonorably."

"What was the offense?" she heard herself asking.

Or maybe she wasn't hearing it at all but was only imagining what she would've asked had she found her voice.

Except that made no sense in light of his one-word answer.

"Murder."

Ten minutes later found Julian in the garage wondering if she'd believed him. If she thought he was trying to frighten her. If it had worked.

Or if she'd blown him off as a fuck-up. He wouldn't blame her if she had, considering he'd done such a piss poor job of losing Benny.

At least she'd found them a car that wasn't going to stand out on the road like a sore thumb.

Or a sore foot, he mused with no small bit of ironic humor while rummaging through the tools in the garage for anything he might need on the road.

He didn't care what Katrina said. She needed stitches. For now, the butterfly bandages he'd used would have to do.

His sewing skills were meant to save lives, not to pretty up an injury. If he got within a meter of her with a needle, she'd need a televised extreme makeover.

He wondered if she'd bother repairing that sort of damage to the bottom of her foot. What he'd learned of her when prepping for this mission told him she'd have scheduled the surgery while on the run for her life.

What he'd learned of her since told him his intel was way off the mark.

High maintenance? Maybe. Spoiled princess? Not that he'd seen so far.

Sure their circumstances were way outside the realm of her norm. But they were also circumstances in which he'd have expected her to show her true colors—and he wasn't talking about that damned irritating parakeet yellow.

Leaving through the garage's side door, he headed back to the house, hoping Katrina had found something to wear and was ready to go, because they needed to move. This delay couldn't be helped, but it had taken time away from putting distance between themselves and Benny.

The quicker they reached the safe house, the fewer complications left in the way of Mick Savin taking out the Spectra IT shooter. The less complications distracting Julian from his agenda, as well.

The biggest distraction of all, the length of Katrina's naked legs in that damn bikini, had hopefully been taken care of by now.

She'd sworn she'd find something to wear, even if she had to dig through Tomas's wardrobe as well as Maribel's, what with Katrina being a nice five-foot-ten and Maribel reportedly eight inches shorter.

One step through the door and into the kitchen, however, had Julian barreling to a stop. Katrina's back was to him as she leaned over the countertop bar separating the kitchen from the small nook with the table and chairs.

She wore a pair of chunky athletic shoes, the left one unlaced and left loose over the thick sock and gauze wrapping binding her foot. Instead of the kimono, she wore a man's white dress shirt, sleeves cuffed to her elbows, hem knotted at her waist.

That left the rest of her, from ass to ankles, in a pair of indigo jeans way too big and obviously belonging to Tomas. She'd rolled the hems above the tops of the shoes and switched her hair from a top-knot to a ponytail.

The look shouldn't have made him hard but it came goddamn close.

The way she'd shifted her weight to her right hip, the way the waistband of the Levi's rode low, the way a strip of smooth skin showed between the jeans and the shirttails had him thinking of handcuffs, silk ties, and old-fashioned hemp rope.

And chocolate chip cookies, as well.

He cleared his throat, held the tool tote he'd scavenged so that it covered his fly, and inclined his head when she glanced over her shoulder. "What're you doing?"

"Leaving Maribel a note and a check for the clothes"—her gaze dropped to the tool tote—"and I guess for whatever else you've borrowed."

"You have your checkbook with you?" A ridiculous thought but the only one that came to mind.

She nodded. "I always tuck my wallet in with my sunscreen and stuff. So I'll have my ID. I keep a spare key, too. That way I don't have to carry the whole ring to the pool."

"Hmph." He crossed to where she stood, set his tools next to her pool bag and a pair of fuzzy pink slippers she'd obviously filched, pulled his money clip from his pocket, and tossed three Benjamins on the counter. "I'll cover it."

"You don't have to do that."

"It's a business write-off. Don't worry about it." He pocketed the rest of his cash. "You have everything? We need to get gone."

"Let me finish this note—"

He pulled the paper from beneath her hand and read.

Maribel,
	I had an emergency and borrowed a few things. The money will cover the incidentals, and there's a

*car in the garage you should consider collateral
until I return yours.*

Katrina

Satisfied, he handed it back. "She'll know your
handwriting?"

"She's worked for me for two years," she said,
tearing the check she'd written from her checkbook. "She definitely knows my checks."

She'd matched his cash outlay to the penny. "I
told you I'd cover it."

"I know you did." She dropped her wallet down
into her tote and met his gaze. "But it was my bad
choice in men that is responsible for this mess.
Allow me to assuage at least a small measure of my
guilt."

Buying her way out of her own bad judgment.
Seems he hadn't been far off his original mark
after all, he mused, offering a shrug that didn't
convince him things were that cut and dried.

Especially since he found himself curling his
fingers over his palm where the remembered feel of
her slender foot nearly choked him. "Your preroga-
tive."

"No, Julian." The smile on her lush lips grew
twisted. "My multitude of sins."

five

A multitude of sins.

What a thing to confess to a murderer—if that's what he indeed was. What, not whom, because she refused to believe she was on the run with a man who held no regard for human life.

If that was the case, why go to the trouble to save hers when he didn't know her from Eve?

No. Julian Samms may have been responsible for people dying, but she would stake what reputation she had left that such incidents were line-of-duty, either military or with the covert organization for which he now worked.

She wanted to know more about him, about this unnamed group that kept tabs on men like Peter Deacon and the nefarious underworld through which his type circulated. Where they wheeled and dealed. Where they killed.

Dear God, she thought, and shivered, rubbing her palms up and down her arms to ward off the chill that had nothing to do with the temperature and everything to do with how unknowingly stupid she'd been.

"Cold?" Julian asked, reaching for the air conditioner controls on the sedan's dashboard panel.

She shook her head, glanced over. "I'm fine. As fine as possible considering this mess I've managed to create."

Julian didn't respond right away and she used the time to study his profile. His eyes, which were hidden behind sleek designer eyewear, dark narrow lenses in high-tech pewter frames. His lips, full yet unsmiling. His patrician nose, which she easily imagined on the silhouette of a statue in Rome.

He had cheekbones to die for, an uncompromising jaw, a warrior's long dark hair.

A warrior. Yes. That was it. That was exactly the man he brought to mind. Fierce and protective and dangerous, yet one she didn't fear. One with whom she felt safe.

One unlike any man she'd ever known—a thought that renewed the prickling sensation of gooseflesh, that roused tingles of awareness, a buzz of inappropriate sexual heat.

"You think you created it?"

"Excuse me?" She'd totally lost the drift of the conversation while indulging in her little chieftain/maiden fantasy.

"You said you created this mess."

"Well, yes." She shifted, cocked up her knee onto the seat and slipped the high-top from her swollen and bandaged left foot with a sharp hiss of breath. "Of all the men in all the cities in all the world, Peter Deacon had to be the one to walk into my life."

Julian snorted, then sobered. "Is that hurting much?"

"Which? My foot or my pride?"

"Your foot."

She nodded. "Throbbing a bit, but I'll live."

She caught the press of his lips as he battled speaking further, caught the surrender in the slack parentheses bracketing his mouth.

She couldn't help but smile when he gave in and asked, "And your pride?"

She shrugged. "What can I say? I've been better."

"Tough break," he said, switching lanes.

She turned her attention to the road and beyond. To the sawgrass prairie stretching into the deceptive nothingness of the Everglades. And because her pride was still an issue, she glanced back and changed the subject.

"Do you like what you do?"

"What I do?"

"Your job. Your career. Your calling."

He huffed, shifted to lean away from her, draped his right wrist over the steering wheel. Interesting, she mused, knowing whatever answer he might verbally offer would never be as telling as the language his body spoke.

Withdrawal. Self-preservation. Solitude.

"I don't think about whether or not I like it," he finally said. "It's just who I am. What I do."

Strange that his thoughts reflected the reverse of hers. She wondered why. "You don't differentiate between the two? The who and the what?"

He shook his head. "It's all the same in the end."

Something in his tone of voice . . ."Is that your choice?"

"What's to choose? You do what you do because you are who you are."

A warrior's sentiment. A man called. A man certain, sure. A man who stirred her blood in ways she could barely fathom. It was so unexpected yet so very real.

She shifted to face forward again, deciding she'd hold up her end of the conversation much better without his profile or the cotton-covered round of his shoulder and biceps in her vision's field.

What she didn't count on was the impact of simply having him near. Drawing a breath that wasn't scented with his clean musky warmth was impossible.

Who needed oxygen, right? She'd simply hold her breath. "I can see that, I suppose. Since I've written one thing or another most all of my life."

He remained silent for several long moments, and it took more willpower than she'd have ever expected not to glance over. It took another whopping amount not to scoot closer to him on the long bench seat.

Finally, he spoke. "Why do you write what you write?"

"Excuse me?" She arched both brows then frowned.

"If you've always written. Always wanted to write. Why your column?"

"Ah," she mused softly, smiled softly. "You don't think gossip and lifestyle observations are real writing then?"

She felt the heat of his gaze, the change in his breathing pattern, in the car interior's temperature, in his body language as he leaned toward her rather than away—they all made his opinion perfectly clear.

"I didn't say that." His voice rumbled deep and low. Intimately low.

It was all she could do to sit still. "You didn't have to. Your silence screams your disapproval."

"It's not my place to approve or disapprove." He checked his mirrors. "I'm not your audience."

"You're right. You're not." But he had issues with her column anyway. She needed to let it go. She really did. But it bugged her to be dismissed without reason. "That's why I'm curious as to the basis of your complaint."

This time she did glance over. It was his left wrist now hooked over the steering wheel, his right arm draped along the back of the seat.

Her peripheral vision picked up the motion of his hand as he flexed his knuckles; his fingertips brushed her shirt collar. She felt the sting of his heat and stayed put.

"It wasn't a complaint," he said, looking at her, his eyes hidden behind his dark lenses. "It was a question."

"A question with an attitude," she said, her chin coming up.

"Really?" His mouth quirked. "You think so?"

"Yeah. I know so. I get it a lot." She moved her gaze back to the road ahead, then turned to stare out her passenger side window, regretting that she'd allowed him to stir her insecurities.

That she'd let him put her on the defensive was bad enough.

"So why do it?"

How the hell had he turned the tide of this conversation to wash over her like this? "Why not? I'm giving a whole lot of readers exactly what they want."

"Whether they need it or not."

"And that's your job? Determining what they need?"

"No. My job is making sure you live to write another day."

"Even though I have nothing worthwhile to say."

"I'm sure you have all sorts of worthwhile things to say."

Argh! Men! "So why am I not writing hard-hitting news pieces, you mean? Instead of fluff?"

"Putting words in my mouth now?"

She practically heard his smirk, so she glanced over; oddly enough, his expression appeared as blank as a slate. He seemed to have snatched her from the jaws of death only to bait her with this maddening conversation. "No. I'm only interpreting your comments based on my experience. You think I'm wasting my time and talent."

"That's your spin."

"And what's yours?"

"I only asked why you've chosen to write what you do."

"Because, believe it or not, I offer an escape to a lot of women."

He muttered in that strange foreign language again. "An escape from what? Bad hair days?"

She was beginning to get a sense of where he was coming from. In fact, she'd bet all the money she had on her that he'd been screwed over by a material girl. "It's a visceral thrill for some. To read about experiences they'll never know themselves."

"And that's what Peter Deacon gave you. Those experiences."

"He did, yes."

"And they were important."

"To the veracity of my column, yes."

"So you used him."

"Yes. I did." She took a deep breath and spit it out. "I purposefully and willingly used a man. I admit it. And I enjoyed it. So stuff that in whatever it is you use for a pipe and smoke it."

Julian wasn't sure why he'd badgered her for the admission except that everything he'd seen of her in action contradicted his wealth of intel.

And everything he'd seen during his stints in Egypt and Kenya made it doubly hard to overlook his instincts about women who put stock in material things. About the damage inherent to greed.

He didn't like to be wrong. He was glad to learn he hadn't been. She was exactly the high maintenance diva he'd been led to believe.

Funny then how he still wasn't convinced. How he didn't want to be convinced. How he wanted her to be different because of how much he wanted her.

At least none of his SG-5 partners were on hand to toss his uncharacteristic behavior into his face.

Julian Samms did not suffer fools lightly. Yet he was on the verge of becoming a big one because his dick had its own hardheaded agenda. "Another case of turnabout being fair play?"

"How's that?"

"He was grist for your fantasy mill, and you gave him legitimacy and . . . whatever."

"We were never lovers. I told you that."

"Knowing his reputation, that's a pretty damn hard story to buy."

"I'm not asking you to buy anything. I'm telling you the truth."

A truth he wanted to believe. The idea of Peter Deacon's hands on this woman turned Julian's stomach in inexplicable ways.

He continued on State Route 9336, driving

through the entrance into Everglades National Park, glancing in his rearview mirror and breathing easier the longer the road behind them stayed clear.

"I hate to be a nuisance, but do you mind telling me how much longer till we stop?"

"Forty, forty-five minutes." Probably closer to an hour considering he wasn't driving the roadster.

"And where are we going?"

"A safe house."

"I see. And we'll be safe there?"

"That's the idea."

"For how long?"

"Until it's safe."

She collapsed into her corner of the front seat. *Yesu.* "Katrina, listen. I really don't know. I won't know until Mick checks back in. Rivers is a blockheaded shit, but he's smart. And he's dangerous."

"I know. I felt the sting of his bullets more than once."

"I'd like to get you to a clinic, get your foot stitched up. But I'm afraid if I don't get you off the street then that foot will be the least of your worries."

"You're welcome to do it yourself."

"Say what?"

"You've got sutures in your first aid kit."

"I don't think you want me to do that. Unless you don't care that your foot ends up looking like Dr. Frankenstein's baseball."

"Well, it is the ball of my foot."

He laughed. He couldn't help it. A laugh that he hoped didn't sound as desperately hysterical as it felt.

"Wow," she said, and grinned. "That was nice. You should do it more often."

"Can't. Would ruin my ruthless bastard rep."

This time Katrina was the one who laughed. "Did you earn that reputation? Or pick it out of thin air for my benefit?"

If they hadn't been traveling well over the posted speed limit, he would've slammed on the brakes, climbed between her spread legs, and shown her what a ruthless bastard could do with a bench seat.

He never should have laughed. That one slip in his armor had stirred the tension inside the car unbearably. He was already running on adrenaline and dealing with close quarters and death's snapping jaws.

He sure as hell didn't need this new intimacy. "It's for my benefit. Not yours."

"How does my thinking you a ruthless bastard benefit you?"

"Because now when I invite you into my bed you'll say no."

"Do you want me to say no?"

What he wanted was for her to take off her pants and sit in his lap while he drove. What he wanted was to take back the admission of wanting her, to regain the advantage lost with the show of weakness.

But he didn't say another word. He couldn't. Not when all the things he wanted to say and wanted to do—to her and with her—would double the trouble they were in, would blur the focus making sure he stayed sharp, would keep him up nights remembering why her type wasn't his.

Thankfully, she didn't seem much in the mood for conversation herself. She simply stared out the window while he took them another thirty-eight miles into the park. A very long, very slow-going thirty-eight miles.

The tension in the car nearly killed him. She was too close for his argument about not being his type to hold. Too strong for a woman he'd expected to be vulnerable when out of her league and her element. Too ready to give as good as she got the way he liked a woman to do.

Wo cao, he thought to himself, knowing the sentiment to be true. He was fucked. The road continued until they reached the fishing camp on Florida Bay. He circled the bait shop and the motel's office, heading for the maintenance shed behind it.

"We're here."

Six

Where they were was the tip of the peninsula, deep inside Everglades National Park. The far end of nowhere. Isolated. Abandoned. Alone.

Funny how she was neither worried nor afraid when either response, both responses actually, would've been understandably appropriate.

Instead, she wanted him to answer the question she'd asked all those miles ago. Because now she could think about nothing but his invitation, whether or not it would come, if it would be a test, an assessment of her character, a challenge, or nothing more than a sexual proposition.

Mostly, she wondered what she would say if and when it did come. Right now? She really didn't know.

Once they'd left the main park road and circled behind what appeared to be a fishing camp, mangroves lined one side of the path, palms the other, creating an effective blind alley.

That was how she felt. That she was traveling forward but with no idea where she was going.

Until today, she'd been so bloody sure.

Now here came this unusual man who, with a few caustic comments, pointed questions, and off-hand remarks had cut to the heart of doubts first stirred when she'd learned the truth about Peter Deacon.

"This is your safe house?" she asked as the trees gave way on one side to more prairie with Florida Bay beyond, and the structure came into view. It looked like the run-down camp's redheaded stepchild.

Ignored and forgotten and dilapidated at that.

Julian scoffed, a humorless sarcastic sound. "And here I thought you more than anyone would know not to judge a book by its cover."

His slams were beginning to get on her nerves. Or maybe it was the fact that he'd wedged up against her defenses that had her on edge.

Then again, it could have easily been the near-miss shootings responsible for her mood.

Whatever it was, she snapped. "It's hard not to in this case. My life is in danger, and those four walls don't appear capable of keeping out the wind, much less any gunshots fired my way."

He didn't even respond. He did no more than park the car, grab the first aid kit and her pool tote out of the backseat, and order her to wait. She watched him cross the dirt drive to the three front steps, unlock the door, and enter.

He obviously felt they were safe enough for her to stay in the car alone, but she still couldn't shake the sensation of being watched.

Ridiculous, she knew, because they were on the tip of nowhere. If any eyes were trained on her, they belonged to Peeping Toms of the raptor or reptilian sort—a thought that had her second-guessing her decision to get out and stretch her cramped legs.

Julian returned less than five minutes later, jogging out to open her door. She swung her right foot to the ground, propped her left on her knee, and eased the shoe back up over the bulky bandage.

The reality of her injury set in when she stepped from the car. Her foot refused to bear but the slightest bit of her weight. She pitched forward, and grabbed onto the car door for balance.

Julian stepped in and wrapped his arm around her waist. "You okay?"

"Uh, not really." The admission escaped with a panicked bit of a laugh. And a wince. "I've obviously been sitting too long."

"Judging by the lack of color in your face, I'd say it's more than that." He muttered under his breath, that weird dialect again. "Let's get you inside."

He bent then, scooped her up like she weighed no more than a feather pillow, kicked the car door shut, and carried her to the shack.

And, oh how right had he been with his reminder that appearances could be deceiving. Once through the doorway, she swore she'd just set foot inside a plush rental on any Florida vacation beach.

The interior was painted a cheery sky blue, the main room's furnishings done in shades of mango, banana, papaya, and lime, the floor in a winter white tile.

"You've got to be kidding me," she mumbled, glancing around at what was truly a cozy little cottage. "This is a safe house?"

"You were expecting industrial cinder blocks?"

Julian's chest rumbled as he spoke, reminding her of their respective positions.

Not that she had forgotten so much as done her best to focus beyond his heat and his strength, his bulk and the sure beat of his heart.

Now that he'd spoken, however, it was all brought back in a sizzling frisson of awareness.

One too powerfully real and compelling to over-look.

For now, however, until she'd had time to process the scope of their situation—the intimacy, the isolation, the fact that he was here to keep her alive and nothing more—overlooking was exactly what she needed to do.

"I guess that's pretty close." She looked around again, took in the brightness, the cheeriness, the plush sofa and side chairs in a print that would pass for African tribal if not for the fact that it was done up in fruit tones rather than rich golds and browns. "I think of safe houses as being dingy and dreary."

"You've been watching too much bad spy TV."

He was probably right—though *Alias* hadn't been the same since Will Tippin's departure. "Uh, maybe you should put me down. Let the blood circulate back into my foot so I can see how bad it really is."

He grunted, carried her through the small house to the bathroom where he'd stashed the first aid kit. He lowered her to sit on the toilet seat and braced her foot in his lap once he'd sat on the edge of the tub.

From the kit he pulled sutures and an antiseptic swab, from beneath the sink a bottle of Betadine. She watched his efficient movements, mesmerized by his lack of hesitation, his certainty, his economy of motion, the wicked concern drawing down his brow.

She looked away from the distraction of his face to that of his hands. Large capable hands with deft fingers that distracted her in ways she preferred he not know. Ways totally inappropriate for the time and place and situation.

Strangely, however, the pain in her foot took away none of the pleasure of his touch. Or perhaps she was able to bear the one because of the other.

Whatever the case, it took her a moment to realize he was waiting on her.

"You ready for this?" he asked. "It's going to hurt like hell."

"I haven't been ready for anything that's happened today." She braced herself with one deep breath, curled her fingers into her palms and dug her nails deep. "This, at least, I think I can handle."

Where the hell was Savin and why hadn't he checked in? Not that Mick would've had time yet to pick up Rivers's trail, but still.

Julian wanted to hear from his partner, needed to hear from the other man, swore if he had to remain isolated for long with only Katrina for human contact he was going to go *kuang qi de*.

And he sure as hell didn't like any of what that said about the self-discipline that had been as much a part of keeping him alive as had his ability to read the people in the crowds he infiltrated.

Reading Katrina was throwing off his plans to hole up, to keep his distance, to wait for Savin to take care of Rivers, then deliver her back to her life.

Dumping the crabs he'd boiled into the sink

filled with the ice he'd picked up during a quick run to the bait shop for perishables, he grumbled to himself. The sick and twisted part of this whole scenario was that reading her should make keeping his distance easier.

But the opposite was turning out to be true. He'd expected to be turned off by the woman who expended creative energy describing the details of her high-maintenance lifestyle for no reason but to feed the fantasies of others.

Instead, he was turned on by a woman who'd shed silent tears while he'd sewn up the gash in her foot.

It had nearly killed him, puncturing her already damaged skin, knowing that he was doing a shitty job because he couldn't keep his hands from shaking.

Some kind of tough guy operative he was. Letting a long tall wisp of a woman knock him sideways.

He tossed the boiled new potatoes into a bowl with salt and butter, sliced the meaty tomato he'd grabbed from the stand outside the shop, and called it dinner.

Katrina was already sitting at the table around the corner, her foot propped up in the seat of the vacant chair to her left, while she flipped through a two-year-old issue of *Florida Wildlife*.

Julian managed to get the food, plates, and utensils, a bottle of wine, and two glasses out of the kitchen in only two trips. Returning from the second, he stopped to watch her situate the place settings as if she were some sort of fucking Martha Stewart.

He dropped the bowl of potatoes with a thud. "We're not usually so formal here."

She shrugged, gave a weak smile. "Old habits. Hard to break."

He grunted. A less than human response but the only one he was capable of making, one appropriate when he considered his vow to keep his distance and his very human weakness making that a hard promise to keep.

He sat down opposite her and tossed her a red shop rag. "I couldn't find paper towels or napkins. I'll pick some up if I make another supply run before we leave."

"This is fine. More practical than wasting all that paper." She spread the rag over her lap like she would a linen napkin then forked up a tomato slice. "Do you think we'll be here long?"

"Shouldn't be. Mick's got a bloodhound nose." Why the hell couldn't she complain about something? Anything?

"Have you worked with him long?" she asked, cracking open a crab leg.

He watched the liquid run over her fingers, expected her to wipe or lick herself clean, groaned when she did neither, when she left the juices glistening on her skin.

He cleared his throat. "Mick? Not really. He was pulled onto the team six months ago. The rest of us have been working together quite a few years."

"Is this a private organization?" She stabbed a potato, bit into the whole of it while it was still on her fork.

"Private?"

She nodded, chewed, and swallowed. "As in not military or law enforcement."

Wo de tian a! "What's with the twenty questions?"

She stopped eating then and met his gaze

squarely, when as fierce as his frown felt, he'd expected her to flinch. He'd wanted her to flinch.

Flinching meant he still held the upper hand, the advantage, was in full control of the situation. Her lack of flinching confirmed his biggest fear of all.

As far as Katrina Flurry was concerned, his control had been shot all to hell.

"I'm making conversation, Julian. That's all."

"I don't do small talk," he said, stuffing an entire potato into his mouth so he didn't have to do talking of any kind.

She tilted her head to one side and considered him. "We could talk about something larger. Nietzsche or Chomsky or Aquinas or Spielberg."

He sputtered. "Spielberg?"

"Ha." She winked, grinned. "Made you laugh."

But he wasn't laughing now. Instead, he was making up his mind whether to eat her for dinner or dessert.

Seven

"Twenty questions isn't such a bad idea, you know," Katrina insisted twenty minutes later as the food—the only real buffer between them—rapidly dwindled along with what conversation she'd managed to force.

Julian frowned, stacked the empty tomato plate on top of his, which now held nothing but a pool of melted butter. "Say again?"

"Something to do besides stare at the walls." Since he was obviously not big on talk of any size, and she didn't think he'd like her spending the rest of the night drinking him in. "The magazines aren't exactly my cuppa tea, not to mention being out of date."

He canted his head toward the living room. "There are DVDs in the bottom of the TV cabinet. No cable, so no reception, but the movies are there."

"As is the PlayStation." Men and their toys. She

cocked her elbow over the back of her chair. "Thanks anyway. But I'm not into video games, anime, or CGI-driven flicks."

"Don't tell me you don't dig Tolkien," he said with a disbelieving snort. "At least this new version. I thought all you women were into the long-haired, pointy-eared British elves."

She shook her head, wishing for *Pride and Prejudice* or *Bridget Jones's Diary*. "My British fantasies are all about Colin Firth. The way he walks. The way he looks into a woman's eyes."

"Sorry." Julian banged more dishes together. "We're fresh out of chick flicks and female porn."

"Don't write yourself off so blithely," she said, curiously pleased when the dishes rattled.

He growled. "What the hell is that supposed to mean?"

Strangely, she was growing rather partial to his surliness. "You cook, you clean. You sew."

When she wiggled her toes, he rolled his eyes. When she winced, he sobered. "You okay?"

She sighed, hating the feeling of being an invalid. "I will be as long as I keep the weight off and the movement to a minimum for awhile."

"Sit still. Let me get the table cleared and I'll carry you to the living room."

"Sure," she said, and nodded, waiting till he turned the corner before pushing out of her chair and hobbling into the other room on her heel.

She lowered herself slowly to the floor beside the coffee table and collapsed back against the couch.

Between the wine- and pain-induced giddiness and the attempts on her life, not to mention the fact that the man with whom she was holed up gave Colin Firth a run for his money, she was feeling rather not in her right mind. Was rather out of sorts, in fact.

Was even wondering if she might not rather sleep with Julian than sleep alone. Sleep as in closing their eyes and not saying a word. Not sleep as in hot slick bodies.

A thought that drew forth the moan she'd been holding back since seeing Julian in that too small T-shirt in Maribel's kitchen.

Or perhaps since the chieftain/maiden fantasy she'd woven as they drove.

Whenever it had happened, she was now suffering from a mighty crush that she feared would bring on more trouble than it was worth. Which was why it would be a monstrous mistake to indulge.

Oh, but how she wanted to, to get her hands on that fabulous hard body, to cuddle up and let him protect her, soothe her, make her sweat.

"If you're not going to sit still and wait for my help, I'm not going to have a lot of sympathy for your pain."

She looked up to where Julian towered above her, his expression fierce, concerned, hard with impatience. "Oh, I'm not in pain."

One brow went up, a warrior who was certain he wasn't being given the truth. "Sounded like a moan to me."

"It was. Just not of the painful variety," was all she said. Against her better judgment, she led him on, teasing, testing the waters, ridiculously turned on when that was the last road she needed to travel.

"I see," he replied, still staring down, seeming to dare her to open her mouth and say more.

A more she wasn't sure of, that made her nervous, that left her with a hollow feeling needing to be filled.

And then he reached into his front pocket, pulled out a deck of cards, and tossed it to slide across the coffee table. "I found these in a drawer in the kitchen. Since my movies and magazines aren't up to your standards, a card game?"

She sighed heavily, picked up the box, turned it end over end on the table. "What did you have in mind?"

"Poker? Blackjack?"

"Stakes?" she asked, one brow raised.

"Since I'm short on cash, it'll have to be clothes."

He was goading her and he didn't know why.

No, that wasn't true. He was goading her because he wanted to piss her off.

If he pissed her off, he'd be guaranteeing she wouldn't want a damn thing to do with him. Right now, that wasn't the case.

She'd had too much wine, was in too much pain, still had to deal with a killer.

And that was the reason—the only reason—she thought she wanted to take him to bed.

He watched her flip the box of cards on the table, from top to side to bottom to side, until it was all he could do not to snatch it out of her hand. Women did not make him nervous.

This one was driving him mad.

No. Forget mad.

He was on a fast track to certifiably insane now that she had stopped with the cards, now that she was worrying her lower lip with her tongue and her teeth, now that she was looking up at him with sleepy-lidded eyes.

"You're on," she said at last, and this time he was the one who groaned. "I'm too muzzy-headed for poker, though. I have trouble remembering the hands as it is."

"Blackjack then."

She nodded; her eyes drifted shut. "That I can probably handle."

"Forget it," he said, and turned to walk off. She wasn't even going to try. She was going to give in, let him win, get naked, and call it a night.

"And here I thought you were the type to enjoy a good challenge," she said behind his back.

If she only knew. The challenge wasn't going to be winning at cards but the end game of turning her down.

"Besides," she went on, "you haven't ever played my version of blackjack."

He turned back, stared down where she rested against the base of the couch, her head back on the cushy seat cushion, one knee drawn up, her injured foot pointing toward him.

He followed the line of her long leg from her foot up her thigh, wishing he hadn't because even in baggy men's jeans she did more for him than a woman had done in a very long time.

"Your version?"

She patted the floor at her hip. "Come sit, and I'll explain."

He tossed the red shop rag he'd used to dry his hands onto the kitchen table he hadn't finished cleaning, crossed the tiled floor, and sat.

Not beside her, though. That would be too close to tempting fate.

Instead, he kept the table between them, draped a wrist over his updrawn knee, and said, "Explain away."

"Okay. I draw two cards from the box and hand them to you. You draw two cards from the box and hand them to me."

"That's it?"

She nodded. "That's it."

"You're making this up as you go along, aren't you?"

"Actually, yes." She tilted her head to the side and considered him from beneath her long lashes, the tips of which brushed her honey blond brows. "I was trying to make it as dangerous as possible. You know. To fit with my life's current theme."

"Katrina," he growled, "what's happening here isn't a joke."

She stared for several seconds, her eyes unblinking, before she hurled the deck of cards toward his head. He caught them, raised a brow, waited.

"I know it's not a joke," she whispered, the sound a raspy sob as she pointed an index finger at his face. "But don't you dare deny me the right to deal with it however I have to. Even if my dealing doesn't follow your rule book for looking death in the face."

Elbows on the coffee table, she buried her face in her hands, her hair, free from her ponytail, falling forward like a concealing curtain. He didn't want her to cry. He sure as hell didn't want to be the cause.

He'd convinced himself she was incapable of taking anything seriously, of giving credence to anything deeper than designer labels. But one by one she was shooting the legs off the ladder he'd used to climb into his ivory tower.

He'd been casting down stones to destroy her façade when there had been no need. She wasn't who he'd thought she was at all.

Unless she was a hell of an actress and he was a big fat sap.

He flipped open the box and knocked the cards loose like he would a cigarette. "You want to pick first or you want me to?"

"You've got the deck. You go," she said, brushing back that mane of hair and looking at him with purely dry and, oh, such wicked eyes.

Sap, hell. He was a fucking puss. He slid two cards from the box, slapped them facedown on the table.

She took the box from his hand and did the same for him. He met her gaze, refusing to check out the cards he'd been dealt. "I win, I want your pants."

"Fine." Her voice didn't even shake. "I want your shirt."

She turned over her cards, the queen and ten of hearts. *"Ai ya,"* he muttered, knowing she'd have no idea who or what he was damning, and flipped his two of clubs and four of spades into the center of the table.

He muttered further while yanking his T-shirt over his head and off. He tossed it beyond her shoulder to the corner of the couch.

And he swore the moment fabric hit fabric, the mood in the room tightened to bursting. As if a ratchet had been applied to the tension and torqued.

Katrina's sleepy, seductive eyes widened, then closed. She pursed her lips, blew out a slow, steady stream of breath. A subtle shudder seized her limbs and she flexed her fingers, and pointed the toes of her left foot.

It was when she looked back at his face that he knew the depth of the trouble he was in. Wine or no wine, pain or no pain, she had sex on her mind.

And not the cheap and quick, any-dick-will-do variety, but intimate and intense sex with him.

"You going to deal or what?" he finally asked, hating the raw sound of his words.

She tapped the box on the table, tugged two cards free and used two fingers to slide them to him facedown. Then she offered the box, which he took, grabbing the two topmost cards and slapping them down for her.

She picked them up, but was a long time looking at them, her gaze wandering instead over his bare shoulders and throat and what she could see of the rest of him with the table blocking her view.

Meat. *Zhandou de yi kuai rou.* He felt like a friggin' piece of meat, and forced his gaze to his hand, which was no better this time than it had been the last.

A five of hearts and six of diamonds. A whopping total of eleven.

Katrina turned her cards over slowly and one at a time. The seven of diamonds. The six of clubs. Besting him by two. *Gou shi.* Shit, shit, shit.

She stared at both hands of cards, worried her bottom lip with the edges of her teeth, finally lifted her gaze, which had grown heated and heavy, to say, "I want the band from your hair."

He blinked, caught off guard, having expected her to strip him to his skivvies. Instead, he tugged the leather band the length of his hair and handed it over, watching her watch the strands brush his shoulders, watching her watch him shove it back from his face.

He couldn't help it. He had to know. "You looking for something in particular?"

She shook her head, grinning slyly. "Just a fantasy I've been entertaining lately."

He snorted, grabbed up the box, handed her two more cards. "Here. Fantasize that this time I win."

"Okay, but you realize I have to take off my shoe to take off my pants, which is an unfair advantage."

Fuck unfair. He just wanted another look at her long bare legs—and was willing to give her even more advantage to make it happen.

"Here." He reached down and slipped off both of his shoes. "I'll give you two shoes to your one."

She didn't even hesitate, adding her athletic high-top to the mix, turning over her king and ace of spades.

He gave a cursory glance to his nine and jack of the same friggin' suit and reached for his fly.

"Wait."

Hands at his waist, he looked up.

"You're still wearing two socks." She made a "gimme" motion with her hand. "One of them will do."

For her, maybe. He was ready to be done with this exercise in bad luck that was dragging out way too long. He wanted to get to sleep because he was not going to bed her.

Still, he did no more than pull off one sock as she picked up the deck of cards.

Finally. He stared at his two tens while watching her turn over two fours. Once he laid his cards down atop hers, she reached for the copper button at her waist, lifted her hips, tugged the denim down and off.

That left her sitting in borrowed white panties that did little to curb his appetite.

They played another round without speaking. Not that either of them had said much at all—a reality that should have made him a lot more comfortable than it did.

Mindless, uninvolved sex he could handle. If he took her right now, that was exactly what he could have. He could get her out of his system and be done with it.

But that wasn't what he wanted. And because he wanted more, he wasn't going to allow himself to do more than look and lust.

He lost his second sock and they played again. This time when he won, he couldn't even gloat because he had no idea what to ask for.

The way she sat now, the elastic legs of the panties teased his line of vision. He could see the edge of one hip before his view was blocked by the bulk of the table.

Taking her panties made less sense than her top, her bra, her one sock, or even the diamonds twinkling in the lobes of her ears.

And so because he was half bastard, half gentleman, he asked for her bra.

"Interesting choice," she said, smiling as she reached beneath her loose shirttails for the back clasp. "Rather safe, yet rather sexy."

"Just working with my own fantasy over here," he said, figuring it was a safe enough admission.

"You intrigue me, Julian Samms. I thought you'd go for the instant gratification of getting me out of my panties."

"Nope." He shook his head, watched her breasts bounce beneath the white oxford cloth, and swallowed hard. "Never been the gratuitous sort."

A smile played over her lips as she reached for the cards. A smile that had him wanting to respond in kind. And to kiss her. And to slit his own wrists for both.

"Whose turn is it?" she asked.

"Does it matter?"

"I suppose not. Since neither of us has much left to lose."

"Really?" he asked perversely, feeling angry and frustrated for no reasons that made sense. Having no one to blame but himself. Wishing they were anywhere else and there for any other reason than the threat on her life. "Nothing much to lose?"

"I'm talking about clothes, Julian," she said, canting her head to one side and weighing him curiously. "That's all."

He didn't say anything, but took the cards she dealt him before choosing two for her. He lost, and waited for no more than the lift of her eyebrow before skinning down his pants.

"Will you do something for me?" she asked as he slid, depending on his luck, what could very well be the game's last two cards across the table. "Will you come to bed with me tonight?"

She turned over the hand she'd been dealt. His knocked them out of the park. Her shirt or her panties. He was clueless on how to decide. "We're not going to have sex, Katrina. Not tonight."

"That's okay," she said, smiling as he showed her his cards. "I just don't feel like sleeping alone. Not tonight. Not after today."

She waited for him to respond, but his throat had swelled to the point that he couldn't even swallow. He thought of holding her close for no other reason than that of her needing him.

It was a thought that left him stunned and with nothing to say but, "Go to bed, Katrina. I'll be in soon."

He got to his feet, helped her to hers, looked away as she limped her way around him in nothing but a shirt that was too sheer and borrowed panties that shouldn't have been the least bit provocative.

He didn't look back until he had no choice. Then and only then did he watch the hem of her shirt flirt with the curves of her bottom, take in the length of her legs, her slender ankles, the way her slow progress never drew a single word of complaint.

Once she'd closed the door to the bedroom, he grabbed up the cards, shoved them back into the box, and returned them to the kitchen where he stood staring at the floor.

In the dark it was so much easier to picture Kenya, and to wonder why the visual memory of the blood he'd spilled—and especially the why—was doing nothing to help him keep Katrina at a distance.

How the hell he was going to get through this mission, he hadn't a clue. He wasn't even sure he was going to make it through the night.

Eight

Katrina lay curled on her side unsleeping, waiting, wondering about the strange game of blackjack she and Julian had played hours ago. Wondering what the hell they'd been doing besides making a bad situation even worse.

Wondering how a game of cards could so obviously be not about winning or losing at all.

She punched her pillow into an even harder knot beneath her head, pulled her knees closer to her chest, winced when she jabbed the toes of her good foot into the ball of the other, elevated on a spare pillow.

Having sat still for Julian's needle earlier, she swore now that she'd make the worst field soldier ever. Focusing on his warrior's face was the only way she'd gotten through the pain.

She had nothing on which to base this visceral attraction. Yes, he was gorgeous, but so had been

Peter Deacon. And she better than most knew looks had nothing to do with who a person was.

What Julian's appearance did, however—because it was more than the set of his mouth, nose, ears and eyes—was compel her to discover what about him left her feeling as if she would never, even with her best years ahead, have time enough to learn all there was about him to know.

He was enigmatic, aggravating, and arrogant. But he was also kind. Very very kind. And funny whether or not he wanted to be. He was serious as the situation demanded, and vigilant, and formidable.

Such simple qualities proved what a good man he was. One more complicated than all the men she'd known combined.

Her eyes were already closed when the bedroom door opened, but still she squinted at the soft spill of light from the lamp left on in the other room. Julian closed the door just as quickly as he'd opened it and stepped to the far side of the queen-size bed.

She realized she was holding her breath, listening for his movements, his bare footsteps on the tiled floor, his discarded clothes rustling. What she wasn't expecting was the heavy sigh he expelled. Or how her heart raced at the feel of his weight settling at her back.

She moved nary a muscle, waiting for him to speak, to fall asleep, to shift closer or farther away. He did none of that. He did nothing at all.

And so she finally turned onto her back and gave a sigh to match his. "I'm not asleep."

"I know." His voice rumbled through the coils of the mattress.

She felt the vibration the length of her spine and curled five of her toes. "Too much on my mind, I guess."

"Your foot?"

She shook her head. "It throbs a bit, but I just took more Advil."

"You've got it propped up on a pillow still, yes?"

She smiled to herself. "Yes, boss."

He grunted.

This time she laughed. "It's okay. I'm so out of my element here I need direction. Even of the bossy sort."

He said her name with a growl. "Then listen to me when I say the one thing you need now is sleep."

"I know. I just can't." Her mind was a jumble of so many thoughts, zipping here, there, everywhere. Coming back always to him. "I need more wine. Or a really good orgasm."

He nearly broke the bed frame turning from his back to his side. "No sex. My rules."

"Oh, I don't need you for an orgasm," she said, digging her own grave even deeper. "And I wasn't suggesting sex. Simply thinking of effective sleep aids."

"Jesus," it almost sounded like he hissed, draping an arm over her middle and hauling himself close. His breath was warm where it stirred her hair when he muttered, "Go to sleep, Katrina."

That might happen if she were to be hit on the head with falling debris.

"I can't." Not with the way he'd surrounded her, his arm, so heavy and warm, the bulk of his body, his face so close to hers. He suddenly seemed much more threatening than any assassin's bullet.

A threat she feared would turn her life as she knew it upside down. "I'm sorry. I just can't."

"You're starting to piss me off here, woman."

Such sweet talk from the man she was falling for. "A bedtime story would be nice. Or even twenty questions."

After a short silence, he said, "Ten."

"Ten?"

"Ten questions. Not twenty." He moved so that his chest pressed her shoulder. "And hurry up before I fall asleep."

She felt as if he'd given her the moon. She also felt as if his skin would set hers on fire.

"Okay, number one." *Think, think, think.* What did she want to know most of all? "Have you ever been, are you now, or will you soon be married?"

"That's three questions," he grumbled.

"Only if it requires three answers."

"Still making up rules as you go along?"

She would've smacked him but wasn't sure he wouldn't smack back. "Answer, please."

"No, no, and no. Three answers to three questions."

She didn't care what he said. She was only counting it as one. Then again, the wealth of information gained was worth letting him keep score.

Now for the nitty-gritty. "Does what you do for a living ever scare you?"

He responded with a snort. "All the time."

"Do you make a lot of money?"

"Scads. Stop being shallow. You just wasted number five of the ten."

She smiled to herself. "I was just trying to figure out why you do it if it frightens you."

"It's more of an adrenaline buzz than true fright."

He paused to adjust his pillow. "Besides, being scared is no reason not to do what you know is right."

Finally. That peek into his psyche she was wanting. "Do you always know what you're doing is right?"

"Does this count as one of your questions?"

She considered only for a moment because this one mattered more than the others. "Yes."

"I wouldn't do it if I didn't know it was."

"Is that why you came after me?" she asked softly.

"Yes. And that's seven."

She allowed a private smile, then sobered. "Do you know why Peter's firm would want me killed?"

"Yes," he said, then said nothing more.

"Are you going to tell me?"

"That wasn't what you asked."

True. She'd only asked if he knew. She felt as if she were wasting her questions, though she was quite sure he wouldn't hold her to the original ten. Not when she had so much at stake and when he didn't have it in him to be that unfair or unfeeling.

She twisted her fingers into the top edge of the sheet. "Why, then? It's not like Peter shared anything about who he was. I don't pose a threat of any sort."

"They seem to think you do. That he leaked information. Or stored it in your place."

"He was never in my place." He'd been arm candy of the cosmopolitan sort. Not her lover. "He did a lot of business in Miami and kept a suite at the Mandarin Oriental. I would meet him in the lobby when we went out."

"I don't need to know the details, Katrina."

"But I want you to know." *Nice. Now she sounded like a shrew.* "I don't want you to think less of me because of lies you've been told about my relationship with him."

"This is a job. It doesn't matter what I think."

"It matters to me." She shoved his arm away, used the heels of her palms to scoot herself up in the bed to a sitting position. "I'm not the bimbo flake you've obviously determined that I am."

"And that bothers you."

"Yes, it bothers me." She was used to being judged by her appearance, by what she wrote, which was often deemed fluff. She wanted Julian to see the truth. "It bothers me a lot."

"Why?" he asked, flopping onto his back.

She was not going to cry. She was not going to cry. "Because I don't want you to feel like you're wasting your time saving my life."

He cursed in that strange foreign language and squirreled around roughly to sit on the edge of the bed. "Don't put that bullshit about one life being worth more than another into my mouth."

His words reverberated in the small room, bouncing from wall to wall like a ping-pong ball. She dodged the impact; the move was too late. The bitterness with which he'd loaded the statement slammed her back.

He hurt. He ached. He lived and breathed a pain unlike any that had hurt her as a child.

She'd lost track of how many questions she'd asked him. It didn't matter; there was only one thing left she needed to know. Had to know.

The only truth that mattered.

"Julian?"

"What?" he snapped, his breathing harsh.

"Who did you kill?"

* * *

Of course he hadn't answered her. He'd done what she'd expected him to do. He'd left the bed, cursing violently—or so she assumed—and left the room.

Following him would've been the wrong thing to do. That much she hadn't needed a crystal ball to see.

So palpable was his anger, in fact, she wouldn't have been surprised had it taken the form of a sentient being. The emotion was that obvious, that very real.

What she didn't know was whether she was the cause. Or if her question had simply tugged on the roots of an event time had long since grown over.

Either way, keeping the width of the cottage between them for the time being had seemed a safe course to stay.

Eventually, she'd slept. Or so she assumed since a pale gray light now limned the shade covering the window above the bed. He'd had long enough to cool off, long enough to brood and to stew.

It was time he got over himself, time he let her in. She wanted her answer, especially considering that after the coast was clear and she got back what remained of her life, she wasn't going to want to let him go.

That much she knew for a fact.

Wearing nothing but the dress shirt she'd had on now for eighteen hours, she slipped from the bed and eased out of the room. The front of the cottage was dark but for a wedge of light casting an eerie glow from the kitchen.

The refrigerator. She'd bet her bottom dollar.

She limped her way around the corner, took in the view awaiting her, and froze. Julian stood in the triangle of the open door, staring at the meager contents, wearing nothing but long-legged boxer briefs.

Oh, for a thousand words.

Seeing the body that had been in bed with her earlier took her breath away. The shoulders and chest, which were broad without bulk. The abdomen, which was flat yet rippled. Long arms, large hands. The leanly muscled legs of a triathlete. The thick package of his sex above.

She didn't want him to know she was there. Ridiculous when he'd probably sensed her stepping from the bed.

Still, he never said a word. And she never moved. Even when he looked up to see her half naked and staring.

He closed the refrigerator door then, silencing the room's grating light and returning the intimate darkness. She heard her own harsh breathing over the quiet, heard his, too, above his footsteps on the linoleum floor.

The rhythm of their heartbeats charged the air in the room, a deep throbbing beat older than man's soul. A powerful, telling beat that spoke of hunger and fear, of life and survival, of love and desperation.

When he reached her, he slipped his hands beneath her shirt, circled her rib cage, lifted her to sit on the countertop, and wedged himself between her legs. He trailed his fingertips over the plump sides of her bare breasts before going to work on the shirt's buttons.

Her hands found their way to his shoulders, her legs around his waist. He kept his gaze trained on his fingers until he reached the last button in the row, the one closing the shirt tails between her legs.

Only then did he look up, the meager light glinting off the blue in his eyes.

The shirt fell open; he spread his palms over her thighs and said in a voice she barely heard for his gruffness, "If you want to stop me, this is the time."

"I don't," she whispered, and shook her head. She didn't want to stop him at all.

Nine

___

Her surrender stripped away what remained of his damaged control. He slept with women he met on the job. Never with women who were the job.

And this was why.

From this moment on the stakes were higher for both of them. He couldn't afford to split his focus. But neither could he afford the price of walking away.

He slid his hands from her thighs, up over her hips and rib cage, his thumbs teasing the outer curves of her breasts until he reached her shoulders.

Once there, he spread open the two sides of the shirt and bared her skin to his gaze. The light wasn't enough to see more than the glitter of the diamonds in her earlobes and her shadowed form, but that was okay.

He saw all he needed to see with his hands. Her

softness, her firmness, the gooseflesh on her upper arms, the cold sweat of her nerves.

He thought about soothing her with the words women loved to hear. How he would never hurt her, how she couldn't be any more beautiful, how he wanted her beyond what he'd known possible.

He didn't say any of that because none of it mattered. The lies overshadowed the truth. He would hurt her in the end. That much he knew to be fact.

And right now was all about loving her body with his.

She sat unmoving, her hands on his shoulders, her heels in the small of his back, her chin lifted, her long neck exposed. He wanted to be everywhere at once, to touch and to lick and to fuck.

He started by taking her shirt all the way off and pinning her wrists to her hips. He liked the idea of immobilizing her; he didn't know why. He also liked how close her breasts were to his mouth, the way she smelled of sunscreen and the sweat of the day.

It was a sexy smell, natural, real. He leaned in, his face between her breasts, and ran his tongue from her sternum to the base of her throat where her pulse beat and her moan of pleasure rumbled.

When he lifted his head, she struggled to free her hands and tightened her thighs where she gripped him. He chuckled against her skin, enjoyed her resulting whimper, then moved to the left and took her nipple into his mouth.

She tasted salty and sweet and he wanted to see her, to know if she was the color of an apricot or a plum. He suckled and tugged, and her low throaty cries tugged at him in return. He felt the pull deep between his legs, felt the blood surge until he thought the head of his cock would explode.

Christ, but this wasn't supposed to happen so fast. This need to bury himself inside of her, to feel the tight walls of her beautiful cunt squeeze him and milk him and drain him until he ran dry.

He moved to her other breast, nipped and licked and sucked and did his best to pretend he was doing so with a nameless, faceless body. One he would enjoy and pleasure but would never see again.

Not one belonging to a woman whose life was in his hands.

He pulled away, let loose a flurry of curses he knew she wouldn't understand. Yet it wasn't until she said, "Julian?" in a voice so soft he melted with it that he admitted to the gravity of this mistake.

And then he did what he had to do.

He kissed her.

He let her arms go, and she wrapped them around his neck, kissing him back like staying alive depended on how well she used her teeth and her tongue.

She used them like a courtesan, a high-paid call girl, yet he knew the intensity of the kiss was real. Whether fueled by lust or driven by fear, her response was genuine and the hottest thing he'd ever known.

He slid his tongue deep into her mouth, seeking to deepen her fire along with his own response. He held her face in his hands, sweeping through her mouth, tasting her, moving closer so that her breasts flattened against the muscles of his chest.

The sounds she made were of heat and hunger, and he growled in return, filling her mouth with all the words he couldn't say, with passion unfamiliar and raw and consuming.

She cupped the back of his head, pressed her

thumbs into the tired muscles at the base of his skull, massaged him there as she pulled her mouth free to kiss his face, his eyelids, the skin beneath his neck.

Enough, he barked to himself, undeserving of her tenderness when this was only sex, not emotion, not feeling, not involvement. It had to be so little. He couldn't trust it to be more.

He pulled free, took his frustration lower, nipping and licking his way from the hollow of her throat down her body, tonguing her navel, spreading her thighs wide with his hands and breathing in the scent of her sex.

She shuddered. From no more than the heat of his breath, she shuddered. Her reaction had him pins-and-needles impatient to witness her come. To feel her pussy contract around his cock, his fingers, his tongue.

He started with the latter, kissing his way up her thighs, left to right, holding her ankles as she leaned back on her elbows, until he reached the soft crease where her leg met her sex.

He tongued her then, licking his way between her swollen lips and finding her clit. She cried out when he drew on the knot with his lips and sucked, a sound of pain mixed with pleasure that had his balls drawing close to his body, his cock surging up to the sky.

He lifted her legs, draped them over his shoulders, and skinned out of his briefs before ringing his fingers around the base of his shaft. He squeezed his cock with one hand, used the thumb of the other to pull back the hood of her clit.

He exposed her to the air and to his mouth, circling the nerve endings with the tip of his tongue until her hips left the countertop and she raised up toward him.

She offered herself fully, and he took the gift, slipping one finger then two inside of her, sucking on the lips of her pussy, her clit, and stroking himself as he did.

He was dangerously close to unloading all over the cabinets and floor. She did that to him, spun him off the axis that had kept him stable since Hank salvaged his sorry wind- and sunburned ass from Kenya all those years ago.

He'd spent the time since embroiled in his work, banging who he could when he could. But nothing had prepared him for this.

He released his cock, slid his free hand up her body to cup a breast, to slowly pinch his fingertips around one nipple. She lay all the way back then, covered his hand where he tweaked her, sent her other hand down between her legs.

She tangled her fingers with his, masturbated, slipping her thumb into her cunt to pleasure herself. He couldn't believe it. Could not believe this woman.

He swirled his tongue in and out and around, wedged her thighs wider apart, pulled her other hand away from her breast and urged her to play.

She snugged two knuckles around her clit, rubbed and tugged and thrust up against him. He slid the flat of his free index finger beneath her pussy, pressing against the entrance to her ass.

She was sobbing now, her head thrashing, begging him to take her, to fill her. He wet his finger with her juices and did, sliding into her slowly as she clenched around him.

She came then, and he'd never seen anything

like it. Never known a woman so uninhibited, so open, so explosive. So much a part of her own experience. Convulsions tore through her; she contracted around both their fingers. Pre-cum beaded on the tip of his cock.

He tried to ease her down slowly, but his own ass was aching from the tightness, the swelling. Sweat ran down the middle of his back as he held his body in check.

But she didn't want to be eased and gentled. She wanted more, telling him so with a gruff, "Move," as she shoved him back with the sole of her good foot planted in the center of his chest.

He stumbled, she jumped down, turned, and bent over. He thought he was going to die. Thought he had when she gruffly whispered, "Julian, please, fuck me."

He cursed, jerked open the kitchen drawer of twine and scissors and electrical tape, searching out the condoms he knew were there.

Once he was sheathed, he took hold of her hips and stepped into her body, sliding himself between her thighs, knowing if he used either of the entrances to her body she offered, he'd be done like a Sunday pot roast.

He breathed deeply, smelled her musk, and hardened further, taking time to wrap a mental fist around his flyaway control.

"Do it. Please. Do it now."

"Let's go to bed. Get you off your foot."

"My foot's fine. Other parts of me are in desperate need of attention. So attend, already."

Though nothing about this was funny, he chuckled. And then he surged forward into her sex, which was wet and hot and amazingly still tight. He pumped as hard as he could, slamming into her.

All the while she cried, "Yes," and "More," and "Harder. Fuck me harder."

It was over almost before it began. He felt the heat of his load burst and turn him inside out. He squeezed the muscles around his ass, dipping his knees to drive into her, realizing that her fingers were buried in the folds of her sex as she brought herself off once again.

He waited through her cries and contractions then pulled free, spun her around, and ground his mouth to hers, kissing her thoroughly until they were both satisfied. And neither one of them could separate his taste from hers.

Ten

She wanted him again. Already. She ached and burned and knew she was torn and raw. It didn't matter. She had to have him again and now.

First things first, however. Taking hold of his hand, she led him through the front room, now bathed in dawn's sunlight, down the hall, through the bedroom, to the bath.

"Wait a sec," he said, disappearing only to return seconds later with a roll of duct tape and two food storage bags.

"You need to keep the stitches dry." He ordered her to sit on the toilet lid while he sat on the tub's edge and took her foot in his lap, slipping both bags over her injury, taping the tops tight to her ankle.

It was a surreal scene, sitting there naked, neither of them acknowledging what had just happened, the organic intensity, the mind-blowing way they'd so thoroughly taken one another apart.

She wondered if he thought less of her because she wasn't the least bit proper when it came to enjoying sex. She tilted her head to the side, studied his face as he concentrated on the task at hand. "I didn't mean to shock you."

"Shock me?" he asked, never looking up.

Fine. Make her spell it out. "The sex."

"The sex we weren't supposed to have?"

"That would be it." The man was a master of avoidance. "Did I? Shock you?"

"Does it matter?"

She jerked her bagged foot from his thigh. "Yes. It matters a lot what you think of me."

He looked at her then, his expression the same one he'd been wearing since she'd met him. The one that made her nuts because she couldn't read him at all.

So she wasn't the least bit surprised when he asked her, "Why?"

She got to her feet, leaned behind him to start the water running in the tub. "For the same reason that I wanted you to know that I never slept with Peter. Because as much as I love sex"—water temperature adjusted, she straightened, stood, looked him in the eye—"I tend to have most of my sex alone. I don't indulge with any man who asks. Only with a man who I can't imagine not having. One who turns on my mind as well as my body."

She swore a pleased smile flittered across his stoic face as he got to his feet. "The best sex always begins in the mind, Katrina. Trust me. There are still a few of us Neanderthal types who know that."

She didn't know what to say. She'd expected him to clam up again, not give her this glimpse of the man he was beneath his warrior's façade. Speechless, yet certain she was grinning like a fool, she stepped into the tub, thankful for the nonslip strips on the bottom, and pulled the lever for the shower.

Julian followed, closing the curtain, handing her a bottle of shampoo. She met his unwavering gaze as she leaned back and wet her hair.

"You know what I would love?" she asked, working up a head of lather as she backed up beyond the showerhead to give Julian access to the spray.

He wet his head and body and came up sputtering. "What's that?"

"Clean clothes. If I'd known we were going to have to hole up in the middle of the Everglades, I'd've packed appropriately while we were at Maribel's."

"Actually, we have clothes here."

His long dark hair reminded her of Johnny Depp in *Chocolat,* Daniel Day-Lewis as the last Mohican, and she couldn't help but blow out a long slow breath. "What sort of clothes?"

He poured a puddle of shampoo into his palms. "T-shirts and sweats. And, unfortunately, nothing in your size."

"I don't care." She nudged him into reverse, flattening her palm in the center of his impressive chest, moving beneath the water to rinse her hair once he was out of her way.

That done, she planted her hands at his waist and danced around him in the narrow space. "Anything soft and cotton sounds like heaven. Those jeans were beginning to chafe."

"I thought you looked pretty damn hot in those jeans with your ponytail swinging," he said, eyes screwed up as he rinsed shampoo suds from his hair.

She caught a quart of water before she managed to close her dropped jaw. "Julian Samms. Are you actually flirting with me?"

He shrugged, reached for the plastic bottle of body wash he'd left on the back of the commode. "Doesn't seem too out of line considering where I've had my hands and mouth."

She felt a blush rise from her toes to the roots of her hair. "I suppose you have a point."

He glanced down. "Nope. Not right now. I'm still pretty soft."

She was not going to rise to his bait, no matter that her heart tingled with his teasing. "Brain sex, huh?"

"Best sex organ in the body."

Hmm. She cast her gaze toward his groin, the thatch of dark hair there where his thick—but soft—penis nestled. "You're right, of course. Though don't discount the other organs you do have."

"I never do."

"And I'm sure all the other women whose lives you've saved have appreciated it as well."

He opened his eyes then, stared down and demanded her attention with no more than the sharpness of his gaze. "I don't sleep with women I'm assigned to. You're the first. And I plan for you to be the last."

She swallowed hard, knowing what he wasn't saying. He wasn't saying that he'd never sleep with another woman. Only that he'd made a mistake sleeping with her. A mistake he wouldn't make again.

What she wasn't as sure of was how she felt about what was an obvious truth.

She tried to casually toss it off. "So, this thing

we're doing here is like those commercials? What happens in Vegas stays in Vegas?"

He nodded. "It can't be any other way."

She sighed. "I guess I thought . . ."

"What? That this was something emotional? Or real? More than an affirmation of life and all that?"

He was right, but it still hurt like hell to hear him say it. After all, he wasn't the one who'd made the mistake of falling in love. "Why me, then? If you don't sleep with the women you're paid to protect, why me?"

"I'm not paid to protect women, Katrina. Not anymore."

She started to write off his comment as semantics but was stopped by the look in his eyes. A look that had her wanting to ask when he'd stopped, why he'd stopped.

A look that reminded her he'd last walked out when she'd questioned him about who he had killed.

She'd bet her last nickel it had been a woman whose well-being had been in his hands. And she wasn't quite sure how that made her feel.

"Okay then. Forget the paid protection. Why me?"

He arched one of those dark warrior's brows. "Because you make it hard to say no."

She sputtered. "That's about the lamest thing I've heard come out of your mouth. And it doesn't tell me a thing."

The brow lowered. Lowered more, deepened into a deadly-looking crease. "You want the truth?"

Why did his tone of voice make her want to tremble, to run, to hide? "The truth is always a good place to start."

"Because you're not who I expected you to be," he said simply.

"Back to that, are we?" she asked, her ire rising along with the shower's steam. "Pretty girl who writes fluff can't possibly have any redeeming qualities?"

A stream of unfamiliar words rolled from his tongue. "Katrina. For christ's sake. You wear diamond earrings to sunbathe."

She closed her eyes, opened them again, set her jaw, and reached for the stud in her left earlobe. Then she grabbed Julian's hand and dropped the earring into his palm. "There. Feel better now?"

"I don't want your fucking diamonds," he said, handing it back.

She slapped at his hand. The earring fell, skittered across the tub and down the drain. It was like watching her connection to Peter and the disaster of the last few months wash away.

She couldn't believe the uplifting sense of relief. She reached for the other. "I don't want them either."

Julian snagged both of her wrists, pinned them to the wall on either side of her head. "Stop it."

"Stop what? Stop doing what I have to do to save my own life? Isn't that why we're here?" She shivered from his heat and his fury, and finally saw herself in his eyes. God, she'd been so stupid not to see it before. "Or is your perception of me as high maintenance giving you a problem with that?"

"You don't know shit about what you're saying, Katrina," he growled down.

She lifted her chin, feeling as if her heart would rumble straight out of her chest. "No? Then why don't you explain it."

"Why don't I just fuck you instead," he said, a nanosecond before his mouth came down.

He tasted like raw anger and unleashed rage, and none of it frightened her at all. This was who he was, a bottle of emotion needing to explode.

And so she let him, matching every stroke of his tongue, every nip of his teeth, every harshly inhaled breath, yet being the cognizant one, the one to finally ease the kiss back from a disastrous precipice.

She struggled against the hold he had on her wrists, demanding he relent. When he refused, her demands became insistent.

She pulled harder, slipping her hands from the vise of his; he flattened his palms against the wall on either side of her head while she wrapped her arms around his waist and pulled his body close.

She angled her head, pushing up into the kiss, feeling the tremors that gripped his body, surprised that he'd revealed himself so, thrilled that he trusted her that much.

She soothed him with her mouth and with her hands, sliding her palms over the hard straps of muscle on either side of his spine, massaging him with her fingertips, the heels of her palms, drawing on his lips with tiny sucking kisses.

He was huge and threatening as he loomed above her, his stance, his bulk, his fierce internal fight that she knew he didn't want her to see. She didn't have to see a thing. She felt and tasted it all, and when he shuddered and gave up one sharp sound that was almost a sob, she swore she fell completely in love with every inch of this damaged warrior.

Her warrior. Her man.

Moving his hands to cup her face, he softened the kiss. She was so glad they were where they were so the tears welling and falling from her lower lids vanished into the water drops beaded on her face.

Whatever he'd seen, whatever he'd done, it was killing him, yet nothing she could say right now would mean a thing because he was a man and he understood the language of sexual intimacy more than he did words.

And so she used her body, her hands, and her mouth, pulling away from his kiss to trail tiny love nips over his throat and collarbone, down the center of his chest to his belly.

He didn't even move. He remained statue still, rock hard and aloof, his hands coming to rest on her shoulders as she pushed back the shower curtain, turned to sit on the edge of the tub, and took his growing erection into her mouth.

He was soft and hard and thick when she took him to the back of her throat, cupping one hand to hold his sac, wrapping her other fingers around the base of his shaft.

She stroked him as she sucked him, the moisture of her mouth and that from the shower creating a slick lubrication, one she used to explore the extension of his arousal where the hard ridge rose behind his balls.

He muttered beneath his breath, sharp foreign words that had her smiling, had him asking, "What's so funny?"

"That language. What is it?" she asked, and went back to circling her tongue around the plum-ripe head of his cock. Oh, but she loved his taste.

"Mandarin."

She grinned again. "As in oranges?"

"As in Chinese. Christ, Katrina. Don't make me talk."

The idea that she could make him do anything thrilled her. And suddenly she didn't want to do this anymore. She was selfish and she wanted more. Wanted the fulfillment of having him inside of her.

With her lips pursed around his tip, she looked up and met his fiery gaze. "Julian?"

He growled.

"Would you make love to me now?"

The words were barely out of her mouth before he reached for her, hooking his hands into her armpits and pulling her to her feet.

His face was set in an expression of hopeful determination, and she smiled at the thought that she'd put it there. But that was all the time she had to think because his mouth was on hers again, his hands on the backs of her thighs lifting her up.

He pinned her to the wall with his weight and drove into her. She tore her mouth from his and cried out, wrapping her arms around his neck and holding on for the ride.

It was fast and furious, his erection stretching her open, his fingers gouging into her skin. She loved it all, the need, the power, the shattered control.

Her sex burned and ached with the friction and the arousal spreading through her like swamp fire, insidiously taking hold until putting it out seemed an impossible task. She would never get enough of this man.

She felt the flex of his legs on the backs of her thighs as he primed himself to come. His pleasure kindled hers unbearably, and she buried her face in his neck and let go.

He followed, and the sounds of their shared pleasure closed around them in the cloud of steam, wrapping their joined bodies in an embrace that felt like forever.

Eleven

Julian held Katrina close in bed, listening for her deep even breathing before gathering up the courage to say what needed to be said.

Earlier they'd finished showering in cold water, then tumbled between the sheets afterward, using one another's bodies for warmth.

At least that's how it had started, a teasing and tickling case of Katrina's shivers, and his selfish intentions to get his hands on her under the guise of rubbing the circulation back into her skin.

But the need for warmth had quickly turned into the need for much, much more. For one another and solidarity and so many things that weren't about the situation they were in at all but were about the two of them as a man and a woman.

He'd made love to her again, the way he'd wanted to from the very start. Slowly. Looking down into her eyes, her breasts pressed flat beneath his chest, her ankles crossed in the small of his back.

He ground himself against her, rotated his hips in slow motion, watched tears leak silently from the corners of her eyes as she'd come.

He was exhausted. And she was finally asleep. But he wanted to tell her the truth.

He wanted her to know who and what he was because the small hold he still had on hope was growing tighter and stronger the more time he spent in her company.

And if there was even the remotest possibility this was more than sex, she had to know everything. Details he'd told no one. Details none of his SG-5 partners nor even Hank Smithson knew.

Spooning up into Katrina's body, Julian wrapped his arm around her middle, tucked her head beneath his chin and breathed deeply. "I was in Kenya when it happened. Assigned to a task force that no one digging through military records would ever find. We didn't exist, but we knew that going in."

He stopped, waited to see if his whispered words had disturbed her sleep, or if he was safe to go on. Her hair, which tickled his nose, smelled like the sea, like fresh air and freedom, and he lay there for long moments and did nothing but breathe her in.

"We were guarding a family of tribal royals from Burundi who were in negotiations to use the port at Mombasa. They wanted access to the facilities they would need to export their coffee beans. We were only there to make sure the meetings happened. No one wanted to see more civil unrest hit the news. Not after Rwanda."

What happened had been more like the chaotic urgency of Somalia and *Black Hawk Down* in the end. But the beginning was the killer. The decision he'd made causing all hell to break loose. The one he would have to live with every day for the rest of his life.

"It happened at zero three hundred," he said, then realized he should back up to make the whole thing clear for her. And for his own piece of mind.

"The wife of the tribal leader never appeared in public without wearing every piece of gold she owned. She knew exactly how dangerous it was but was too arrogant to care. I hated that bitch. She was bad news from day one."

Which was why he'd taken her on as his personal project. He'd been determined she wouldn't fuck up an assignment that should've been as simple as a baby-sitting job.

"It was the last night before they crossed the border and our services would no longer be needed. They refused to stay in any of the villages where shelter had been offered, so we pitched tents every night. And we traveled at a snail's pace because the elders couldn't handle anything more."

He stopped because he needed to breathe. He swore he hadn't talked so much at one time in years. He liked privacy. He liked silence. He liked sticking to the business at hand. Getting in, getting it done, and getting the fuck out.

He sure as hell did not like spilling his guts. But then, that's what had started this all, wasn't it?

"It was the middle of the night. I heard a struggle and a muffled scream inside her tent. One thing she had made sure I understood was that she never entertained overnight guests." He huffed his disgust. "She had also made sure I knew I was the exception.

"At first I thought the noises were a ploy to get me inside. She was like that. Manipulative. Entitled. But when I went in to check it out, I saw it was nothing like that at all."

He was suddenly cold, and pressed his thighs closer to the backside of Katrina's, wrapped his chest around her body, seeking comfort, a sensation so unfamiliar he almost couldn't breathe because of the way it raced through him.

"She was holding a kid, threatening him with a knife that would've scared the shit out of a butcher. He was probably ten or twelve but looked like six. And he had his hands wrapped around a dozen of her bracelets."

Even now he heard the woman's words, heard her cold orders. *Kill him. Kill this thief now or I will gut him and leave him as carrion for the scavengers. And then I will do the same thing to you.*

She would have done it. And suffered no consequences. In an ugly twist of fate and foreign policy, the camp of tents was considered a mobile embassy, the inhabitants subject to diplomatic immunity.

That didn't mean he'd been able to let her.

He'd looked into the child's eyes and seen desperation, but nothing even resembling fear. Nothing resembling hope. Whether he died of a knife wound, a bullet, starvation, or disease, he would die. And he knew it.

"I took him out," Julian whispered, and choked. "Had one of my men help me dig his grave. And then I shot him because it was the right thing to do. I turned myself into my superiors after that. The end of my military career."

And the beginning of another once Hank Smithson had gotten wind of what had gone down.

Julian turned onto his back then, flung his forearm over his eyes and waited for the sweats to begin. For the aftershock of reliving that night that had defined his life. Of having to live with himself since.

But they didn't come. And his heart didn't throttle like an outboard motor. Neither did his muscles seize up and burn. Even when, at his side, Katrina stirred.

"I didn't know they grew coffee in Burundi," she said softly, turning over on the mattress and into his arms, drifting in and out and only hearing part of what he'd said.

And that was okay. She didn't have to hear it all. It was enough that she'd responded to his voice. That she was here.

He held her closer than he'd ever held another woman in all of his life. And he didn't even flinch when she whispered, "I love you."

The words settled into his skin and soothed instead of stinging like he'd braced himself for them to do for years. It was a ray of hope strong enough to slash across his darkness, and it made him smile.

It was midafternoon when Katrina finally woke for the day. Had she been at home, she would have headed to the gym, where she would sweat and ponder her column due on Monday.

As it was, she was pretty much assured she'd never have a deadline again.

Strangely, that didn't bother her at all. Not after the incredible twenty-four hours she'd just come through. She was aware now like she hadn't been before how little what she did for a living mattered. Or how being alive was nothing compared to feeling alive.

Escaping a killer's bullet had helped her make the distinction.

Falling in love with Julian Samms had defined the differences in the subtlest of ways.

She pushed up and swung her legs over the side of the bed, surprised to find the flow of blood into her foot hurt less than she'd expected. Surprised, as well—and pleased—to find a clean white T-shirt, socks, and gray athletic sweats on the foot of the bed.

She hobbled her way to the bathroom and did her thing, glad to find the borrowed panties she'd hand-washed last night dry enough to wear. She dressed and exited ten minutes later to find a steaming cup of black coffee on top of the bedroom's dresser. *Oh, wow,* she thought, smiling like a crazy woman to herself.

What she didn't find was any sign of Julian, though she swore she'd heard him talking. And swore his voice was coming out of the bedroom wall. Coffee in hand, she stepped across the room and slid open the door to the closet.

The interior wall was actually a panel that hid a tiny hutch of a room where Julian sat in front of an electronic console, a set of headphones held to one ear.

He glanced her way, held up a finger signaling her to wait. She nodded, stood in the entrance, studied the bank of high-tech equipment that was like nothing she'd ever seen.

No, that wasn't true. She had seen one similar. In a movie. On the command deck of a spaceship.

And that's when it finally hit her. The truth

about Julian Samms. Who he was, who he worked for. It was all so far and above anything she would ever understand. A truth she would probably never fully know or even grasp if he told her. Told her . . .

What was it that he'd told her during the night?

She frowned as she sipped her coffee, certain she'd heard his voice, picked up random words, though she'd never surfaced to grasp what it was he was saying.

What she had latched onto was the feeling in his tone, the emotion behind the confession. Yes, confession. She was sure that's what it had been.

And looking at him now, even with the fierce expression casting shadows over his face, she sensed that his spirits had lifted.

Whatever it was that had happened beyond the incredible sex, she was glad she'd been there for him.

"Right," he finally said, adding, "I'll be in touch," before dropping the headphones to the surface of the desk, where he propped his elbows before burying his face in his hands.

She moved closer, ducking beneath the low-hanging entrance to place her palm on his shoulder. "Are you okay?"

He swiveled his chair toward her, grabbed her by the hips, and pulled her between his spread legs. When he lifted his gaze, she braced herself, one hundred percent certain she wasn't going to like what he had to say.

"Mick's been shot."

"What?" Her heart bolted to the base of her throat. "Who?"

"Rivers."

"Where is he now?" she asked, not even sure which man she meant.

Julian didn't wait for her to clarify. "Mick's safe. He'll be fine. But Rivers is on the loose."

Twelve

Katrina didn't know what to say. Knowing what to say depended on knowing how to feel.

How she felt was numb.

Or at least that was her initial reaction. Moments later the reality set in along with the cold sweats and the nausea.

Her stomach burned and heaved. Her throat ached. Her foot throbbed.

She'd been expecting to be a free woman in another few hours. Maybe a day. Maybe two.

As long as she'd known Julian's partner was on her shooter's trail and she was in capable hands, she'd been able to convince herself she'd be out of harm's way soon. Back to Miami. Back to her life.

Now, however, she was able to convince herself of only one thing. She was going to be sick.

She bolted for the bathroom and dropped to her knees. Her coffee cup slid from the counter where she'd set it into the sink with a clatter. Eyes closed, she grabbed for her hair, and that was it.

What she'd swallowed of the coffee came up along with remnants of last night's crab dinner. She retched, heaved, and spit her way through the process of her stomach turning inside out.

Humiliation blazed—she didn't want him to see her like this—overshadowed only by an angry fear. How dare these people ruin her life when she was only an innocent bystander?

Minutes later, Julian was on the edge of the tub at her side with a wet cloth. She lowered the toilet seat and flushed, collapsed back against the wall where she let him bathe her face, thinking that no man had ever done this for her.

That there had never been one she had wanted to. One she would have allowed to.

"Thanks," she said, taking the rag and opening it up over her face. Hiding behind it and wishing for a magic toothbrush to appear.

"I can make you some tea," he suggested tentatively. "Some toast."

She nodded, smiling, pulling the cloth away. "Tea and toast would be nice. Thank you."

He shrugged one broad shoulder. "Sounded like a girly sort of thing to offer."

She smacked him across the shin with the wet cloth for being such a man. "Are you calling me a girly-girl?"

"Get over it. I like you that way." Hands on his knees, he got to his feet. But he stopped before leaving the room. "I do like you, you know."

"I should hope so," she said, because flirting was easier and healthier than panic. And because flirting with Julian felt right in ways she'd either forgotten or never had known.

"Katrina, I'm not going to let him get to you."

She stared up into his gorgeous eyes, eyes brimming with an emotion he couldn't hide. Tears welled and spilled from her own in response.

And this time it was the fear of losing the man she loved to a killer's bullet that had her hugging the commode.

The front door had opened and closed before Julian registered that the sound had come from the other room and not from the toaster behind him.

He was in the kitchen scavenging for a pink or blue packet of artificial sweetener, and had decided Katrina would have to settle for sugar in her tea when he heard her go out.

Unless what he had heard was someone else coming in. *Tzao gao.* Shit. He didn't figure Rivers for that dumb. Katrina on the other hand . . . and his SIG was hanging on his chair in the comm room.

He dashed through the house, snagged up his holster, slipped it on, and hurriedly reversed direction, hitting the outside steps in time to see her top half disappear behind the car's open back door.

She scooted out, turned to sit on the bench seat as he jogged down the steps toward her. He swore she was going to fry what was left of his patience. "What the hell are you doing? Trying to get us both killed?"

Her gaze came up sharply. Hurt at first, then mad. "I only wanted the house shoes." She had her hands wrapped around the fuzzy pink slippers she'd brought with her from Maribel's house. "I'm about to kill myself in those bulky sneakers."

He reached in and grabbed her upper arm, forcing her out of the car. "You don't leave the house, understood? You want something from the car? You tell me."

She jerked away, opened her mouth to obviously give him an earful, never got out a word. The car window shattered all over the both of them.

Julian shoved her back, dove into the car on top of her. He went for his gun; she grunted as his elbow caught her solar plexus. Then she scrambled into the floor behind the driver's side seat before he could say a word.

At least a word in English, yelling, *"Liukoushui de biaozi he houzi de ben erzi,"* just as the rear windshield exploded. Glass pellets burst inward. Katrina screamed and covered her head.

Her forearms took the brunt of the blast. Blood peppered her skin where she was hit. She whimpered softly but didn't move, didn't speak, didn't even breathe.

He needed to draw Rivers away from the car, away from Katrina. He bailed into the front seat, kicked open the passenger side door. He pressed his head back into the headrest, counted to ten.

"Rivers! We need to talk."

He turned to glance over the seat at Katrina—just as Benny answered with a single red dot of his laser sight on Julian's white T-shirt. He ducked, but it was too late.

The shot came through the driver's side window, lifted him off the seat, and slammed him to the ground. The last thing he heard before darkness took him was Katrina's scream.

And Benny Rivers's hollow laugh.

* * *

Julian came to to searing light in his eyes, searing heat swarming over his body, and searing fucking pain ripping his shoulder apart.

He squinted, grunted, winced, and unscrambled what he could of his brain. Rivers. The gunshot. Katrina. *Qingwa cao de liumang.* He struggled up to his good elbow . . . only to realize he wasn't wearing his shirt or his holster.

And that he wasn't alone.

Crouched on the ground beside him was a man packing supplies into Julian's first aid kit. He blinked, focused, stirred to the fact that he'd been wrapped up and taped up and put back together again.

Just like Humpty Dumpty.

He cleared his dry throat. "How bad is it?"

"You were two inches away from needing your shoulder rebuilt." The man, his dark skin glistening like coffee beans in the sun, zipped up the canvas pack. "That'll hold you until you get to a hospital."

Julian shook his head. "No hospital. I've got to go . . . somewhere."

"Then I hope to hell you have another way to get there." Squatting now, his wrists dangling over his knees, the man nodded toward the borrowed car. "Rivers did a number on your spark plug wires."

Julian turned his head slowly to take in the other pieces of the V8 engine strewn on the ground like so much litter.

He had to find Katrina. With Mick out of commission and the trail gone cold . . . He needed to get inside, raise Kelly John or Christian. There had to be word on the wires about Rivers.

Rivers . . .

Pushing to sit upright, Julian turned back to his visitor and sized up the other man who knew way too much about Katrina's assassin.

His reflective sunglasses and combat boots, weathered skin-and-bones appearance, his dreads tied back in a black bandanna, and the Tac-Ops Tango 51 slung across his back—it all said one thing.

Julian had just hit a big fat dead end. A road-block worse than any he'd erected to keep those who tried to get close at a distance. His partners. Hank.

Katrina.

Didn't matter much now. He wasn't going to have much of a life left once this man was through with him. Though why he'd patched him up first . . .

Julian frowned, said, "You're Spectra."

The man nodded, stood, shook a dark cigarette from the thin square box he pulled from the pocket of his black T-shirt. He offered one to Julian before firing up the lighter he dug from a webbed pouch on the leg of his khakis.

He drew smoke into his lungs and blew out a long slow stream, then stepped back and kicked Julian's SIG across the drive.

"Hell of a situation here, isn't it?" he said, bringing the cigarette to his lips again.

The hell? Julian stared at the gun as if seeing a mirage before picking it up, scooting back against the car, holding his injured arm close to his body.

His palm scraped over gravel and broken glass, but his gaze never left the other man's face. And his hand never left the gun. Even though it had been freely given.

Spectra was just as good at taking away. "Do you know where he is? Where he took her?"

From another pouch pocket, the agent pulled a GPS locator. "Looks like they're back in Miami, man."

Christ! He'd been out that long? "What do you want?"

"Me?" The man shrugged. "I want Rivers."

Julian levered himself to his feet using the sedan's door frame. "What're you doing here then? If you want Benny?"

"I figured you might want the girl." He filled his lungs one last time then flicked the cig to the driveway and ground out the fire with his boot heel. He then picked up the first aid kit and nodded toward the house. "You wouldn't have a beer in there, would you?"

Julian nodded because he was hurting too bad to think straight. He needed a whole lot of answers but couldn't come up with a single coherent question.

Holding the elbow of his busted-up arm with his good hand, he made his way to the front steps, wondering what the other man knew of where he was and who he was tangling with. Wondering if at this point either of them cared.

After all, they were about to share a beer.

"There's a six-pack in the fridge." Julian indicated the kitchen. "I'm just gonna . . . get another shirt."

Gritting his teeth as he hurried down the hall to the bedroom, he grabbed a T-shirt from the closet, stepped into the communications room, and as quickly as he could with one hand, typed the security code to launch the program he needed.

Another few seconds of using only his index finger to hunt and peck out his message to the SG-5 ops center, and he was done. He secured and shut down the system, secured and backed out of the room—right into the cold beer bottle the Spectra agent held out for him.

Having hooked the earpiece of his sunglasses over his T-shirt's neckband, the other man inclined his head toward the concealing door now sliding shut. "Nice setup."

"Yeah. It's not too shabby." Julian took the beer, and led the way back to the front of the house once he heard the click of the lock on the comm room door.

With a loud grunt, he lowered himself slowly to the sofa's edge and struggled into the shirt, sweat running from what seemed like every freaking pore on his body. He'd forgotten the pain of the gunshot.

He didn't like remembering. "You've got a tracking device on Rivers, right?"

"Actually no." The agent sat across from Julian. "It's on your girl."

"Katrina?" His pulse raced against his fast-tracking thoughts. No wonder they'd never been able to shake Benny. But how . . .

His head came up. "The earrings."

A knowing nod. "Deacon wanted to keep her in line. Who'd've figured they'd come in so handy, eh?"

Nothing here was making sense. "Why the hit on her?"

"Hell, man. There's no hit on her. That's all Rivers's paranoia." The man sat forward again, spun his beer bottle back and forth on the coffee table. "He did a lot of off the books work for Deacon. Stuff the bosses are interested in."

"And he's taking out Katrina before she can talk." *Ta ma de hun dan.* He wasn't going to let that happen. He was not going to lose this woman now.

"Not if I get to him first, my man."

Julian pushed to his feet and met the other man's gaze directly. "You know she doesn't know a thing."

"Yeah." A nod, another cigarette worked between two fingers. "She's been on the radar for awhile. Bosses know she's clean."

That was good. That was good. But it wasn't enough. He needed to make this one thing crystal fucking clear. "You so much as look at her the wrong way after this and I'll shove that rifle barrel up your ass and shoot you myself."

"I'll just bet you would," the agent said as he stood, his dangerously soft laughter rising with him, though never reaching his eyes.

Weird or not, he was Julian's best hope for getting out of here and getting to Katrina. "What're you driving?"

"Ah, my man. A Baja Outlaw." He winked. "Docked in the marina. We can blast around to Key Largo and up to Biscayne Bay."

Julian nodded, figuring how much time he needed to get out of the house, down to the docks, into the water. Calculating the equation on his way to the door, he punched the resulting instructions into the electronic keypad above the deadbolt.

This place had been the main source for monitoring Spectra IT's Caribbean activities for years now. But not anymore. Not after being compromised. He walked out, grimacing with every step as he followed the agent to the docks.

They were well into Florida Bay headed east when the explosion rumbled around them, shooting a fireball like a rocket into the sky.

He saw the reflection in the lenses of the other man's sunglasses, accepted the silent but smiling

salute as the agent touched a finger to his forehead before throttling up. And as he did, Julian
caught a glimpse of the ring on his finger.

A ring worn only by graduates of the United
States Naval Academy.

Thirteen

South Miami, Saturday, 9:30 P.M.

Katrina sat on her balcony's rough pebbled surface, the sharp edges biting through her sweatpants into her butt, her hands tied to the railing behind her, her foot throbbing like the head of a child's squeeze toy, while inside, Benny Rivers trashed every room in her house.

Her split lip tasted like blood and still ached from where he had backhanded her hours ago. Eyes closed, she banged her head against the iron bars behind her because her position didn't allow that she kick herself in the ass for ever getting involved with Peter Deacon in the first place.

At least she finally knew why she was going to die. It made the idea of ending this very bad weekend with a trip to the afterlife easier to take. Okay. That was a lie. She was scared shitless but had no more tears to cry. She'd cried them all out over Julian.

Or so she'd thought . . . but here they came

again. Oh God. Huge tears running unchecked in rivers down her cheeks, soaking the neckband of her T-shirt, which had only just started to dry. She saw him lying on the ground, blood pooling dark and thick and red around him.

How could anything hurt this badly? So very very badly. Losing the man she wanted in her life before she'd had a chance to know him. Or to tell him. *Dear God,* she sobbed, her stomach so tightly wound she had to fight the burn of the nausea threatening to double her over. What must her mother have gone through when her father had died?

She stopped her self-induced concussion and stared up at the stars, thinking of what a hero her father had been, how he'd come to her rescue all those times when she'd been threatened with disfigurement by the girls who didn't want her hanging around their boyfriends. Or ignored by the teams who wouldn't choose her to play because girls who looked like she did couldn't throw a ball.

She missed her father so very much. She missed her mother, too, and couldn't believe she would never see her again. Would never have a chance to say good-bye. And now her mother would have to hear about what happened from halfway around the world. This was all so incredibly unfair. So very wrong.

She flinched at the sound of more glass breaking inside. She'd always loved the privacy her condo's balcony offered, how she was able to enjoy her evenings out here, unwinding with a cold drink and a good book, but right now she wished she lived anywhere else.

Closing her eyes, she did her best to put the horror of the present from her mind and think back to the cottage, imagine living there with Julian. Loving there with Julian.

Until meeting him, she had never believed anything more than attraction happened at first sight. Now she knew the truth. How two souls destined to share their lives knew it the moment they met.

And in that second, with that thought, at the very meeting of the two, her eyes flew open, her stomach quit aching, her mind began to spin.

She had to get free. She had to get back to the safe house. She had to find Julian. See for herself if he truly was dead, or whether he was still lying on the ground, abandoned, alone, and waiting for help.

The thought of him injured and helpless. Hanging on. Hoping. She had to get to him. She refused to sit here and go quietly into that good night without seeing for herself that he wasn't alive.

She had to get loose, get to her gun, and rattled the rails behind her. "Hey, Benny. Come here, will you? I need to talk to you."

A minute later, the short bulky man loomed over her in the open sliding glass doorway. "You better be ready to say something I want to hear."

She nodded, didn't even have to fake the tremors in her voice. "Peter gave me a flash card. He told me to keep it safe. I think it's what you want."

Benny snorted. "And you're just now remembering it? I don't think so, sister. This sounds like some sort of game to me."

"It's not a game. I swear." But it was. A game of playing for time. Of dealing hands of lies. Of dodging and feinting and rebounding from more of his heavy-handed blows. She swallowed hard, knowing what was coming. "I carry it in my wallet."

He stared down at her as if processing what she'd said, then turned to look inside. "I've turned this place over and haven't seen a wallet any-where."

She swallowed again and braced herself, wondering if it would be a fist or a foot, praying for neither. His insults were so much easier to take. "It's not here. I left it back at the motel."

His head swiveled back slowly, like a piece of heavy equipment operating in slow motion. And then he reached into his pocket, pulled out his handkerchief, and gagged her. "Now why the hell would you do something that stupid? No, don't answer. Let me tell you. You're a stupid female. Damn breeding bitch."

He kicked out with all the strength of his bull-in-a-china-shop bulk behind the blow. She cowered, cringed, but it didn't do a bit of good. He aimed the toe of his shoe at the ball of her bandaged foot, and she swore she felt every one of Julian's stitches split open.

She screamed, the sounds absorbed and muffled by the fabric ball in her mouth. She willed the nausea down while working to dislodge the gag with her tongue. Choking to death was not part of the plan.

The click of Benny's knife had her screwing her eyes all the way shut and doubling over. Instead of stabbing her in the back, however, he reached down and sliced through her bonds before jerking her to her feet.

She stumbled inside, hopping on one foot, dragging the other behind her like some nursery rhyme sheep. Mary? Bo Peep? She couldn't remember. And the fact that she'd tried to spoke to her state of mind.

Looking around at the devastation of her things, she leaned her weight against her sliced and shredded sofa, rubbing the circulation back into her wrists, unable to care about anything beyond getting away.

Benny slid the patio door closed and charged into the room. She glanced quickly away from the hutch on that same wall, thankful that he didn't seem to have found the hiding place where she kept her handgun.

He grabbed her upper arm and shoved her forward so hard she nearly stumbled to her knees. "Let's go."

She tried to talk around the handkerchief, ask him to let her change her clothes, go to the bathroom, wash her face—anything to put him off from leaving before she could get her hands on her gun. But all that came out of her mouth were gagging, muffled sounds.

"Yeah, yeah. You keep talking," he said, dragging her down the tiled foyer toward the door. "And I'll keep enjoying not listening to your fat trap of a mouth."

He pulled open the door and jolted to a stop, brought up short by the gun barrel inches from his face. Katrina's heart thundered in her chest.

"Going somewhere, Benny?" asked the dark-skinned man holding the very big handgun with the futuristic laser sight and extra long silencer on the end. "Or should I say, going somewhere without me?"

Benny jerked her in front of his body like a

shield, his meaty hands wrapped around both of her wrists where he held them in the small of her back. "Get the hell out of here, Ezra. This is between me and her."

"Wrong, Rivers," said another voice from the hallway, a smoothly rough voice Katrina would've recognized anywhere, one that had her knees shaking to bear her weight. "This is between me and you."

She cried out with joy and sagged against Benny's hold as Julian stepped around the corner. He was pale, his shirt matted with wet and dried blood, his mouth bracketed by lines of what had to be excruciating pain.

But he was alive, and she cried again. Relief, fright, hope. She couldn't define any emotion but love.

"Let her go, Rivers," Julian demanded, never meeting her gaze. "It's over."

"The hell it is." Benny hefted her up as best he could—she was four inches taller and not giving him any help—and lugged her dead weight back the way he'd come, pressing the tip of his knife blade to the base of her throat as incentive.

Her eyes went wide with the sting of the prick. She felt the warmth of the blood trickling over her skin, grimaced as Benny tightened his hold and growled in her ear. "Walk, bitch. I'll cut you open to your gullet if you don't."

He backed her into the wall beside the balcony exit and stopped, breathing hotly into her ear as he ordered, "Open the goddamn door."

She reached around his bulk and slid the door open, her gaze locked on Julian where he stood in the foyer's shadows.

Ezra had moved into the living room, his gun aimed at Benny, the red dot of the laser hitting Katrina in the eyes as Benny jerked her around. "The girl isn't part of this, Rivers. You know that. You fucked up. Peter found out. Now you have to deal."

"Forget it, Ezra," Benny yelled, the knife slacking, his voice cracking once as it did.

That was enough for Katrina. She reached for the edge of the hutch as if needing the support, flicked the switch hidden under the center molding, and held her breath as the lock on the sliding drawer released.

She felt the pull of Julian's gaze then, and looked over to see the subtle, imploring shake of his head. He could beg. He could demand. It didn't matter.

She wouldn't survive Benny's knife or the fall from the balcony to the ground. She knew she would be facing one or the other once he dragged her out the door. She had to do what she had to do to save her own life.

She took a deep breath, counted to three, drove her elbow into Benny's midsection. He grunted, loosened his hold. She grabbed for her weapon, swung it down behind her, and fired.

His howl of pain and rage took the roof off the room. She dove for the floor. Ezra fired. Benny went all the way down. And then Julian was there on his knees, helping her pull the gag from her mouth.

"Oh, God. Oh, God. You're alive." She touched his hair, his face, his neck and chest and hands. All the places she could get to while avoiding his gunshot shoulder. "I thought he killed you. I thought you were dead." Her voice was a wet soggy mess. "I just found you and I thought you were already dead."

His big broad hand came up to cup her nape. He pressed his forehead to hers. "Shh, Katrina, sweetheart. I'm here. I'm fine. I love you."

"Oh my God, Julian!" She bawled because she couldn't do anything else. Her chest ached and her throat burned and her mouth would barely work around the words she'd been holding back far too long already. "I love you, too."

"Yeah. I know that part," he said, and she couldn't decide whether to kiss him once or kiss him forever.

And so she kissed him twice, holding him tightly as they helped one another back to their feet.

"How did you get here? What happened at the safe house? And who is he?" Arms around Julian's waist, she nodded toward the mysterious Ezra. "Should we call the cops?"

"No cops. I'll take care of it," Julian said, and she didn't need to know anything more.

Stuffing portable equipment of the medical sort back into his copious pockets, Ezra got to his feet from where he'd been kneeling next to the unconscious Benny, checking vitals, tying tourniquets, saving her would-be killer's life.

He dusted his hands together, straightened the bandana wrapped around his dreads. "You wouldn't happen to have a wheeled duffel big enough, would you?"

He wanted her help with Rivers? The sound that came out of her mouth was half gasp, half laugh. "For him?"

"Yeah." Ezra shrugged as if he were discussing a bale of hay. "I can carry him out of here, but get-

ting him down the dock and into the boat migh
be more tricky."

She didn't care. She wanted him gone. "I don'
have a duffel but I do have a bicycle trailer."

Julian turned to her. "You do?"

She nodded. "I even have a bike to go with it
They're in my storage unit." When both men stared
at her silently, expectantly, she shrugged. "I'll ge
the key."

She hurried to the kitchen, grabbed the key
from the hooked plaque inside the pantry door. I
was when she turned to go back that she found Ju
lian blocking her path.

"Who *is* that man?"

Julian reached up, stroked her hair back from
her face. "He saved my life. And he's going to take
Rivers out of here. That's all that matters."

It wasn't all that mattered. She wanted to know.
Needed to know. But the details could wait.

She reached up and kissed him, gently telling
him with her lips how much she loved him, and
how exquisitely happy she was that he was alive.

"Now *that* is what matters," she said once she'd
kissed him thoroughly, grinning as he removed
her other earring, his eyes twinkling as he did.
"Okay, okay. That, too."

He hooked his good elbow around her neck; she
wrapped both arms around his waist, never wanting to let him out of her reach again. They headed
back to the living room where Ezra had trussed
Benny like a rodeo calf with a cabled rope he'd
pulled out of his magic pants.

He grabbed hold of a section he'd left for a handle and dragged his load to the door. She nodded
at Julian when he glanced down, then stepped
back and crossed her arms over her chest.

She waited while he talked to the other man, watched while he walked him to the door. He left Ezra there with a salute and a pat on the back, and, as she watched, dropped her spare earring deep into one of Ezra's pockets.

Epilogue

South Miami, Sunday, 4:30 A.M.

"I'm really a much better housekeeper than this," Katrina said hours later, cocooned in her bedroom quilt on top of her mattress, which looked like it had suffered the wrath of a crazed saber-toothed cat.

Once Ezra had dragged Benny out the door, she and Julian had put what they could of her bath and bed to rights. They'd cleaned up together, doctoring cuts, changing dressings—her foot, his shoulder, which was in much worse shape, but for which he refused to see a doctor—checking wounds for infection, downing antibiotics from the life-saving first aid kit he never went anywhere without.

Having her hands on him then as well as now meant as much—if not more—than being alive for him to get his hands on her. She loved being alive to feel his skin, the tremor of weakness he'd tried to hide, the way he had finally and truly relaxed for the first time since she'd known him.

She laughed at that, realizing that she'd known him for less than forty-eight hours, when it felt like he'd been part of her life since the day she'd been born. Well, not quite that long, she admitted, admitting as well that she wasn't ready to give up the dramatic giddiness. Delaying a return to reality as long as possible held immense appeal.

"What day does Maribel come anyway?" Facing her, Julian snuggled deeper into the covers. "This place is a dump."

"Oh, thanks." She started to tickle him, stopped because she sensed how much pain he was in, and stroked her hand down his chest instead, threading her fingers through the dark silky hair that swirled there. "I'll call her later and see about getting your car back."

"Okay."

"Uh, and check into replacing Maribel's?"

He nodded, stroked the hand of his good arm over the curve of the breast he could reach until she shivered all the way to her toes. "I'll take care of it. Business write-off and all that."

She would've glared at him, but his eyes were closed, making it a waste of good pique on her part. Besides, he was fairly mellow—a situation she doubted would come around again any time soon considering how he was always so "on"—and she wasn't above using his down time to pry.

"Julian?"

"Katrina?"

"Thank you."

"For?"

"Saving my life," she whispered.

His fingers, resting on the mattress, teased her navel. "All part of the job, ma'am."

"I know," she said, not even sure she could put

what she was feeling into words. "But I hate thinking that you went above and beyond because of me."

His hand stopped moving at all then. His lashes fluttered; his lids opened slowly. The look in his eyes, even in her barely lighted bedroom, could never be mistaken for anything but what it was.

Julian Samms was mad. "What the hell are you talking about?"

She drew her own fists close between her breasts. "Just that I wasn't thinking. When I went out to the car. Or, I was thinking, but only about my foot. Not about our situation. I had gotten so wrapped up in what we'd done"—she couldn't believe it; she was blushing—"that for that one moment, I didn't even stop to consider the where and the why of being with you."

It was several seconds before he answered. Several seconds during which she feared confessing her alarming lack of vigilance would be the death of the very fantasy—*Julian and Katrina sitting in the tree, k-i-s-s-i-n-g*—that had been the impetus for the destruction all around them.

When he did speak, however, his words, but especially the emotion behind them, were not at all what she'd expected to hear.

"I know," he whispered, his voice rough, rife with a sense of failure. "I'd gotten sidetracked, too."

She blinked; how could he think he had failed? "You were?"

And it was then that she realized he wasn't mad at her at all. He was mad at himself. And his sigh, when it came, was heavy with it. "I heard you go out the door and wanted to kick my own ass. Not for letting you distract me, but for *being* distracted because I knew better. I *know* better."

Uh-oh, she thought, tingles of alarm centered in the small of her back.

Julian went on. "But later, on the ride back with Ezra, I realized it wasn't the fact that I'd let down my guard that was eating at me. It was the reason *why* that I couldn't get over. The same reason I'm here now."

"Which is?" she asked, almost unable to turn the words boiling in her throat into sounds. *Please, please, please, God. Don't let him go.*

"This isn't easy for me, Katrina," he said, taking a deep breath. "Admitting that I'm not enough by myself. That being on my own isn't how I want to live. That I need someone else with me."

Oh, God. Oh, God. She didn't know what to think. What to say. How to respond. Especially when she swore she couldn't tell if he was the one with misty eyes or if she just wasn't seeing things straight.

She didn't think she'd seen anything straight since meeting him. But she didn't care. Not if it meant having him in her life forever.

"Would that someone be me?" she finally squeaked out.

He nodded.

"Because you love me?"

He grinned. "Yeah. And admitting that's the easiest thing I've done in awhile."

She couldn't help it. She giggled. "Then say it again."

"Sit in my lap first," he said, shifting his hips to prod her with his penis, which had grown erect.

She shook her head. "Don't even think about it, mister. You're hurt."

He rolled over onto his back, wincing as he gave her full access. "I'll be hurting more if you don't."

And only because she wanted him so very very

much, loved him so very very much, did she follow
his instructions to the letter, deciding she could
get used to being ordered around if it meant giving them both this much pleasure.

Eyes closed, Julian pulled in a hiss of a breath as
she settled over him. The tendons in his neck stood
out in sharp relief with his strain for control. "Don't
move. Don't even think about it. Just sit there like a
good woman for a minute or two or forever."

Male chauvinist man that she loved. Oh, but he
felt so good when he filled her. When he loved
her. Though, sitting still was probably just as hard
on her. "I sit here much longer, we could starve,
you know."

His eyes flew open. The grin that spread over
his face was the final straw in securing her heart.

"Oh no, we won't." He patted the mattress
above his head with one palm, searching for the
pillows and slipping his hand beneath them.

He rattled what sounded like plastic, way too
pleased with himself as he found the secret stash
he was looking for. "Here ya go."

And then of all the things he could have done,
he fed her a chocolate chip cookie.

If you liked this Alison Kent book,
try the others featuring
the sexy men of SG-5 . . .

AT RISK

Bad Boys. Good spies. Unforgettable lovers.

One of the Smithson Group's elite force, Christian Bane is also the walking wounded, haunted by his past. Something about being betrayed by a woman, then left to die in a Thai prison by the notorious crime syndicate Spectra IT gives a guy demons. But Christian has his orders: Pose as Spectra boss Peter Deacon. Going deep undercover as the slick womanizer will be tough for Christian. Getting cozy with a beautiful suspect, Natasha Gaudet, to get information won't be. But the closer he gets to Natasha, the harder it gets to deceive her. Now, with Spectra closing in, Christian's best chance for survival is to confront his demons and trust the only one he can . . . Natasha.

At the sound of footsteps on the stairs, he swallowed his adrenaline-hyped heart, turned slowly, and watched Natasha descend. Earlier, she'd looked like the epitome of a corporate professional—or that had been his impression, seeing her climb down from her SUV before she'd been hit with Ferrari fever.

But now . . . Now she was all woman. Soft and flowing and female, the hem of her dress swinging around her knees and giving him a nice long look up her skirt at her bare thighs as she made her way down.

He walked toward her, toward the base of the staircase, settling one hand against the balustrade's finial as he waited for her, this nine-lived chameleon who was to be his guide. The heavy flow of his blood through his veins told him how clearly he was anticipating time spent in her company.

And he'd be lying to himself if he denied the source of the tingling buzz at the base of his spine.

He wanted to take her to bed.

She smiled down at him, skirt flaring, hair swinging, and the tingle took on an electric heat.

"I hope you haven't been waiting long."

Just long enough to regain his bearings, he mused as he shook his head. "It's been worth it."

"It's been worth what?" she queried, coming to a stop two steps from the bottom of the staircase.

Two steps that put him eye level with her chest. She was breathing as hard as he was, and she wasn't wearing a bra.

"Watching you." He waited a moment then gave a small nod. "Nice dress."

Her cheeks bloomed a soft pink; she tucked her wrap tighter around her arms and shoulders. If she was trying to blame her body's response on the room's temperature, he wasn't buying it. He'd followed her approach and knew exactly when her nipples had tightened.

"Thank you. Wick enjoys a more formal dinner hour. Or two." She canted her head and considered him. "You look quite dashing yourself."

He'd changed his shirt, added a tie, still wore the black pin-striped Armani and the boots. He hadn't bothered to shave. "Dashing. Hmm."

"You don't think so?" she asked, her grin getting to him.

"I don't think a lot about how I look." Aw, shit. *Character, Bane. Play the part.* Who knew how much her godfather had told her about Deacon's obsession with fashion and style? He moved up onto the step that separated them, ran a hand along the railing until his fingers touched hers. "Why waste the time when I can enjoy looking at you?"

She left her hand where it was, even as he waited for her to back away. She didn't, and in the

next second she lifted two of her fingers, the first
and the second, so that the tips brushed the vee
between his forefinger and thumb.

"What's that they say about flattery?" she asked
with a gently teasing lilt to her voice.

"That it's going to take me where I want to go?"
Boldly, he moved his free hand beneath her wrap
and settled it on the swell of her hip. She was soft;
she was strong. He felt both in the long lean curve
of her body. He felt her tremble, as well, and the
tingling at his spine bored inward.

She cleared her throat, her eyes glowing brightly.
"It might. Eventually. But right now, Wick is expecting us."

"And what Dr. Bow wants, he gets." Wasn't that
what she'd said?

"Something like that," she responded, though
she didn't move.

Christian did, raising his hand at the same time
he lowered his gaze. He measured her ribs with his
fingers, her ribs that expanded around her lungs
and her deep labored breaths. When he reached
the plump side of her breast, he stopped, his thumb
resting beneath the full lower curve, stroking in a
downward motion when what he wanted to do was
stroke up.

"We could skip dinner," he suggested, his gaze
returning to hers at half-mast as she leaned into
the motion of his hand.

"I don't think that would be a good idea," she
murmured.

"Why? Because you don't want to disappoint
your godfather?"

She gave a noncommittal shake of her head.
"That's part of it."

Christian's hand stilled. "Are you afraid of him?"

"Not at all," she said, her voice low and breathy. "Why would you ask that?"

He wanted to know what hold Bow had over her, the extent of her loyalty. How far she would go. He wanted to know if she was playing a part even now, or if what she was feeling was real, because that raw tingling buzz was now poker hot and flaring toward his groin.

He captured her gaze as he moved his thumb, this time in an upward sweep, over the firm swell of her breast to the center, where her nipple stood beaded and taut. His own breathing uneven, he said, "Does he punish you if you disobey?"

She laughed at that, then pulled in a harsh breath when he moved his thumb in a circle. "Wick doesn't punish me. He would reprimand me if he felt he had reason. But I don't give him reason."

And there was Christian's answer to the question of Natasha's loyalty, though the flush to her face, the glassy brightness of her eyes, told the truth of her conflicted desires. "I think you should give him one. Tonight. With me."

"I would never have taken you for the type to enjoy punishment, Mr. Deacon."

"Peter," he said, and tightened his hold on her ribs. The fire in his belly burned like coals from hell. "Call me Peter."

"Peter, then," she said, sliding her hand from the banister to rest on the back of his. "We should be going."

"After dinner, then," he pressed. He wasn't through with her yet. Not halfway through. But the break would give his blood time to return to the head where he needed to be thinking. "You *are* at my disposal?"

of the frightened girls melts Eli's armor, and soon, they find that the best way to survive this brutal assignment is to steal time in each other's arms . . .

DEEP TROUBLE

The Beach Alibi

Ultimate spy Kelly John Beach is in big trouble; during his last mission, he was caught breaking into a Spectra IT high-rise on one of their video surveillance cameras. The SG-5 team has to make an alternate tape fast, one that proves K.J. was elsewhere at the time of the break-in. The plan is simple: someone from Smithson will pose as K.J.'s lover, and SG-5's strategically placed cameras will record thier every intimate, erotic encounter in elevators, restaurant hallways, and other daring forums. But Kelly John never expects that "alibi" to come in the form of Emma Webster, the sexy co-worker who has starred in so many of his not-for-primetime fantasies . . .

The McKenzie Artifact

SG-5 operative Eli McKenzie was in deep cover in Mexico, infiltrating a Spectra ring that kidnaps young girls and sells them into a life beyond imagining when someone on the inside poisoned him, forcing him to return to the Smithson Group's headquarters to heal. But his quick departure led Spectra operatives to nab a private investigator named Stella Banks. Eli knows the only way to save her life is to reveal himself to Stella and get her to trust him. Seeing the way Stella takes care

And no admission that Dr. Jinks was being held against his will.

Christian tightened his hold on her waist, determined to get to the truth. He turned toward her, one hand slipping around to her back and pulling her close, the other moving up to cup her jaw, her cheek, his fingers sliding into her hair. Her gaze grew sleepy, sexy. Her lashes fluttered down, then back up.

When she smiled, he felt it in the palm of his hand as deeply as in his gut, and swore her pleasure at the physical contact was only part of it.

Her enjoyment of the secrets she kept was the rest.

He touched his thumb to the corner of her mouth. "I hope I'm responsible for this."

"Oh, you are." Her smile widened.

"But?" he asked, since he sensed it coming.

"But I'm afraid it's not what you think."

He stroked the line of her jaw. "You know what I'm thinking?"

She nodded, briefly catching the lower edge of her lip with her teeth. "You're thinking that my working for Wick means I know all about his business."

"And you don't," he said, moving his hand to her neck to measure her pulse, which beat hard and fast. Not with the sure, steady pace of a consummate liar.

"Trust me. I'm no more involved with the lab work than Wick is with balancing his accounts." She took a deep breath and a distancing step away. "I hope that doesn't disappoint you."

"On the contrary," he said, returning his fists to his pockets. "It will make it much easier for us to separate business from pleasure."

"Absolutely."

Her husky affirmation even more than her smile nearly sent him to his knees. What the hell was he doing? What the hell was going on? *Play the part, Bane. Play her and play the part.* This game wasn't about getting laid. Yet even as he served up the reminder, he slipped his hand around to the small of her back and pulled her flush to his body.

To Peter Deacon's body.

His mouth was but inches from hers when he said, "After you."

She took a deep breath and blew it out with a light shudder as she made her way to the foyer floor and stopped. "I'm sure by now Wick and Dr. Jinks are wondering where we are."

Christian stopped beside her, saw her mouth move, saw the sweep of her long dark lashes, saw the tiny flare of her nostrils—and saw all of it in slow motion.

What had she just said? "Dr. Jinks will be joining us?"

She frowned up at him. "Wick invited him, yes. I assume that won't be a problem? It is his project you're here for, isn't it?"

"You know about Dr. Jinks's project?" Christian swore his heart was seconds from bursting in his chest.

At his side, Natasha shook her head, confusion creasing her brow. "Not the details, no. I do know that he's finishing up the beta testing of what he's been working on. The timing is why I made the connection between the two of you."

The timing. Right. Not that she had been aware beforehand. Not that she knew the details. Not that she was up to her eyeballs in this scheme along with her godfather.

bracing his forearms on his knees and lacing his fingers into one big fist. He hung his head, but she wasn't fooled for a minute.

He exuded the same tension she saw in the set of Hank's shoulders, the deeply creased furrows lining his brow.

The room, in fact, fairly crackled with the buzz of expectant anticipation. As if what hung in the air was a suggestive truth neither man wanted to address for fear of offending her beyond repair.

And suddenly she knew. She knew. The inappropriate request involved this man at her side.

The very man who all too frequently played a part in her dark-of-the-night fantasies. She wanted to shiver with the possibilities, but instead she tamped down a response that she feared would strip away her current advantage.

Especially as there was a little bird telling her she needed to hold onto all that she could.

"Well, now that you've warned me, I'll have to admit a rather prurient curiosity. This is hardly what I expected."

"And you shouldn't expect it. No woman ever should." Hank leaned back in his chair, laced his hands over the slightly rounded rise of his stomach. "And I suppose we could call off this whole kit and caboodle right now. Save us all what might turn out to be an uncomfortable circumstance."

At her side, Emma heard Kelly John blow out an audible breath. The sound of a scoff. A surrender. A pox on the situation that had brought them here.

She half expected him to push from the chair and walk out of the room, but he sat where he was and said nothing. Nothing to counter Hank's suggestion. No offer of another.

but only to herself, wishing like hell that she could step into this meeting on a more even footing.

But such was not to be when one wore hot pink Spandex. Even had she been wearing the pieces of her work wardrobe she'd had on earlier in the day, the balance would have leaned heavily in the male favor. As was too often the case.

"Sit, Emma, please," Hank requested once she'd reached his desk. She hesitated briefly, but it was enough to broadcast her discomfort at the disadvantage. He picked it up and added, "Let's all sit."

Emma took the seat closest to where she stood, Kelly John the one nearest the window. Hank dropped into his executive chair and braced his elbows on his desk, steepling his fingers as if the pious gesture would lessen the inappropriateness of the request.

Because the way both men seemed reluctant to speak to her or each other, or to meet her inquisitive gaze, she was certain inappropriate would barely cover what they wanted her to do.

She cleared her throat. "You mentioned overtime?"

"Overtime, yes. But this time it's more than my dad-blamed habit of procrastinating on paperwork." Hank paused, and color bloomed in the apples of his cheeks. "As a matter of fact, it's overtime giving you legal grounds to charge my sorry hide with sexual harassment."

"Oh, really," she said, blinking away the strangest sensation of being caught up in a fog-like dream. Even the words he'd spoken were weirdly surreal.

Hank Smithson had never, in the five years she'd worked for him, come close to crossing such a line.

At her side, Kelly John shifted to lean forward,

Not the image reflected back at her from the glass door to Brighton's ten minutes ago. The image of a woman who had spent the last hour sweating like a politician caught with a cigar and an intern.

Oh, well. An emergency was an emergency, even if she was wearing white cross trainers and slouch socks, hot pink Spandex shorts and sports bra, and a white pullover worthy of a wet T-shirt contest.

Not exactly an outfit conducive to professionalism. At least at this late hour, her boss should be alone.

He wasn't, of course, which was bad enough. Even worse was the six-foot-two, two-hundred-ten-pound, blue-eyed, black Irish reality of who was leaning on the edge of his desk.

One very sexy Kelly John Beach.

She placed her satchel on the thick carpeting just inside the door and crossed the expansive office, refusing to adjust her clothing or touch her hair, or give into any of the copious nervous reactions to being seen at her absolute physical worst by the very man she most wanted to attract.

He was one of Hank's special Smithson Engineering project consultants. A group of men rarely seen around the office, but causing all tongues belonging to female employees to wag when walking through.

All tongues save for Emma's. In her position as Hank's assistant, wagging was unacceptable. She didn't speak out of turn. Ever. A well-known and well-documented fact that had helped land her this job.

She wondered for less time than it took her to reach Hank's desk if Kelly John was involved in the request for her overtime. The grave look the two men exchanged answered her question. She cringed,

Emma Webster had just packed up her Billy Bag satchel when the private line on her desk phone rang. It was six-thirty P.M., and she'd thought the office empty.

She'd gone down to the health club at five, had a quick salad at Brighton's after working out, then come back upstairs to grab the novel she'd been reading at lunch before finally heading home.

Instead, she picked up the receiver on the third ring. It was Hank, and if he was still here and looking for her, her cell would be ringing next. "Emma Webster."

"Emma. Hank here."

"Hank. I thought you left hours ago."

"I was called out for a bit"—he cleared his throat— "and I'm afraid I've had an emergency of sorts dropped into my lap. I'm going to have to ask you for some overtime."

"I'll be right in." She took a deep breath and conjured up the image she'd checked in her cheval mirror before leaving her apartment this morning.

he didn't want to hurt her and that gave her an advantage in their wrestling match.

Her mouth landed on his throat first and she licked the salty taste of his skin, groaned, and bit his chin.

"Goddammit . . ." He sounded very uncertain, pained, and he grabbed her other wrist. "You little—"

Her mouth smashed up against his. They both froze, but only for a second. Slowly, deliciously with a purr of excitement, Ariel licked his lips. Her heart threatened to break through her ribs, it drummed so madly.

He brought her arms behind her back, but that only pressed her breasts to his chest, and since her dress hung open, she could feel his heartbeat, as wild as hers. She caught his bottom lip in her teeth and nibbled, all the while breathing hard with excitement, expectation.

And then he exploded. From one second to the next he'd been held immobile by her brazenness. But it wasn't in Sam's nature to be docile, to let anyone else take the lead.

Ariel found herself plastered against him from groin to breasts while his mouth opened over hers in ravenous demand. His tongue thrust in and he groaned low in his throat, the vibrating sound thrilling her.

He slanted his head and drew her even closer, still holding her hands behind her, straining her shoulders, almost lifting her off her feet. Her head was pressed back, leaving her mouth open and vulnerable to his. His whiskers scratched her chin, his erection pressed into her soft belly, and he tasted so good she didn't ever want him to stop.

remaining cuts and scrapes. She didn't want to be a wimp in front of him. She didn't want him to feel sorry for her.

He finished off by applying ointment and some bandages. Then he backed up. "All done. Now."

"Now what?"

"About this . . . wanting me business."

There was nothing she could do but wait and see what he had to say.

Sam floundered, but finally bit out, "Wanna tell me why?"

"Why what?"

"Why do you want *me?*"

Amazingly enough, when she came to her feet Sam backed up. Silly man. "Why wouldn't any woman want you?"

"Ariel . . ."

She took two steps toward him. He took one more back, then planted his feet and refused to budge.

"You're smart and dedicated and heroic and . . ." She shrugged, inching closer, more determined than she'd ever been about anything in her life. "You really are so damned sexy."

She'd gotten close enough to touch him. Lifting one hand, she reached for his shoulder.

He snagged her wrist, his warm, strong fingers wrapping around the delicate bones. "Don't curse. You're too young for that."

Enough was enough. She'd warned him, but he persisted in throwing her age in her face. With a smile of warning, she grabbed his neck with her free hand and went on tiptoe to reach his mouth.

"*Ariel*—" He tried to lean back, to turn his face away. But she backed him to the counter and there wasn't much room for him to maneuver. She knew

Sam leaned forward and blew his warm breath over her knees.

A new ache filled her, one of overwhelming sexual hunger. She'd wanted him since the first time she saw him. She remembered that moment in vivid detail. Pete had taken her with him to his family's regular Sunday get-together. A storm had knocked a thick elm over in his middle brother's backyard, damaging a fence. Sam was there, shirtless, sweaty, tanned, and so sexy she'd stood dumbfounded for several moments while he swung an ax, cutting up the fallen tree alongside his brother, Gil. The muscles in his strong back had flexed with each movement. His biceps bunched and knotted. His hands were big, lean, his strength undeniable.

"Ariel? You didn't faint on me, did you?"

Taking a breath, she opened her eyes and locked gazes with him. He had one hand on her thigh, holding the ice pack there, the other gently touching her chin. The breath sighed out of her. "I want you so much."

He lurched back as if she'd kicked him, jerking to his feet in a rush. "You look besotted, damn it. Knock it off."

She couldn't reply, could only stare at him with all the love and hunger she felt plain in her eyes. *Please,* she silently pleaded, and got a wary frown from him in return.

"Here's a new rule. You have to be quiet while I finish this up. Understand?"

She stared.

"Answer me, damn it."

"Yes, all right."

He moved back to her cautiously. "Give me your elbow."

This time she bit her lip when he swabbed the

None of this was what she'd expected. Not that she'd known what to expect, but worry over a few paltry bruises . . . She heard him returning and quickly replaced the ice pack, wincing at the bitter cold.

He eyed her when he reentered, his expression stern. "I hope you learned a few things tonight."

"Yeah, that you're surly when you're hurt and that you don't like women coming on to you."

He moistened a gauze pad with antiseptic and again knelt in front of her. "Wrong. I'm not all that hurt and I love when women come on to me. I just don't like little girls flirting when they don't know what they're getting into."

Seething, Ariel said, "If you don't stop accusing me of being a child, I'm going to—" She screeched when the antiseptic hit her scrapes, burning like a brand. Her legs stiffened and her hands gripped the sides of her seat.

"Sorry." For once, his voice was gentle, caring.

equals big problems. It may be a rigid rule, but it works—until Pete decides he wants to push the line and transform himself into the perfect guy he thinks Cassidy wants.

THE WATSON BROTHERS

My House, My Rules

Sweetly sexy and extremely determined, Ariel drives tough, rugged cop Sam Watson over the edge. When Ariel's headstrong ways nearly wreck one of Sam's sting operations—ruining her dress in the process—he offers her a ride to his place to clean up. But Ariel seems to have her own agenda, and Sam decides it's time to show the lady that if she wants to play games of seduction, he'll be calling the shots . . .

Bringing Up Baby

Gil Watson's wild night on a business trip two years ago resulted in a daughter he never knew he had. Now that the girl's mother is gone, he wants to do right by his little girl, even if it means a marriage of convenience with the woman who's been raising her. Anabel Truman is totally wrong for him. But the sensations she rouses in Gil feel totally right.

Good With His Hands

As best friends, Pete Watson and Cassidy McClannahan have a "no sex" relationship. "No sex" equals continuing friendship. "Ohmygodyes" sex

And keep an eye out for Lori Foster's
THE WATSON BROTHERS,
coming in September from Brava . . .

Her back straight to the point of being stiff, she crossed one leg over the other, laced her hands over her knees and said, "Actually, I'd like to hear everything."

"You sure?" Hank asked, giving her one last out.

She nodded. "You would hardly go so far out of character to suggest anything improper if you didn't feel it your best option."

That said, she waited, watching the glances that passed between the two men. The silent conversation—*Are you sure? I don't know. Is there any other way? None so simple.*—left her sitting literally on the edge of her seat, swinging her foot, nervously waiting for the balloon to pop.

It was Kelly John who pricked the fragile skin.

"I've gotten into trouble with one of my assignments. And the most convincing way for me to get out is to have you pose as my lover."